SANDRA CARMEL

EVERNIGHT PUBLISHING ®

www.evernightpublishing.com

Copyright© 2025

Sandra Carmel

ISBN: 978-0-3695-1337-3

Cover Artist: Jay Aheer

Editor: Melissa Hosack

SANDRA CARMEL

DEDICATION

For those who have discovered the recipe for delicious, satisfying second chances...

SANDRA CARMEL

Sandra Carmel

Copyright © 2025

Prologue

San Destino community social media page, 9:00 AM, 21st March 2024

<u>Duty Manager required</u>

- Providence Pier, San Destino (Hospitality & Tourism)

- Exciting new work environment with opportunities for growth and development.

- A welcoming and supportive culture, built on collaboration and respect.

- Flexible working arrangements.

- Become an integral part of the team at the newly renovated Lovebirds Bar, previously Providence Pub, as our brand-new duty manager.

- Submit your application to: LovebirdsRecruitment@gmail.com

Chapter One

Las Vegas, 31st October 2003

Gabe Raven stood, dripping with sweat, in front of the cozy, quaint, hot-as-hell, Las Vegas chapel. Alone. Waiting. Like standing in a fire pit, the soles of his shoes almost melted into the scalding pavement. The place had nothing on the stunning chapels back in his Scottish homeland. But he didn't care.

He scanned the busy strip and swiped the persistent stream of perspiration from his brow with his still white-as-fuck forearm. He'd met the woman he wanted, over and above all others, and that was all that mattered. Once he had her permanently, he could embark on their future together. From that point on, he could make the decisions that suited him and Tessa, no one else.

Forced to leave his high school sweetheart two years ago and relocate with his parents, he'd vowed to keep in touch. And he had, religiously. Except her mum and dad hated him. They hated his no-bullshit personality, his family's blue collar, military background, his desire for their daughter.

How many times had they implied—because no way in fuck would they ever be so rude as to admit it to his face—that he wasn't good enough for Tessa? And never could be.

Had he let that deter him? Fuck no. The only person who could convince him to back off and move on was her. Only her. So they'd written regularly, spoken on the phone intermittently—when her parents hadn't intercepted the calls—about their hopes and dreams. They discussed opportunities to be together again, as soon as practically possible, without interruption.

Without interference.

The sun beat down on him, the temperature soaring to what felt like one-hundred-and fifty-degrees Fahrenheit. His t-shirt and jeans stuck to his sweaty skin, but it was a small sacrifice. He could put up with any discomfort, because she was coming.

2:00 PM.

3:00 PM.

4:00 PM.

What had he said in the letter? Meet at 1:00 PM if she agreed to tie the knot, if she knew, like he did, that they were destined to be together, soulmates.

He checked his watch for the millionth time. She could have been held up by flights, her parents. How long should he wait? He'd stated clearly that if she didn't come, he'd know she'd decided against eloping. Nineteen wasn't too young to get married, right? Not when they knew they suited. Unless she'd decided against *him*.

5:00 PM.

6:00 PM.

He'd run out of bottled water and his mouth had dried to beyond parched, his skin bordering on blistered lobster-red. However, if he left the agreed spot and she showed up… Gabe didn't want her to think he'd changed his mind, but if he didn't rehydrate soon, he'd fucking collapse and be shipped off to hospital.

At 7:00 PM his ego finally accepted she wouldn't arrive, had chosen *no* to his proposal. And the realization fucking stabbed him like a blunt paring knife to the heart. Going by their past correspondence, he'd honestly believed her coming was a no-brainer.

Slowly, reluctantly, tail between his too-sure legs, he walked the short distance to his hotel and entered the closest door, the foyer bustling with people, and slammed into a wall of cool, artificial air. Fake, like everything else in this place.

How could he have thought it'd work? Outside of allowing them to virtually marry on the spot, Vegas didn't have the right vibe. It didn't reflect the depth of them and their relationship. He could see that so clearly now. He wished he had before, wished he hadn't pushed for a quick binding, impersonal ceremony.

In hindsight, he'd done it all wrong. Had her parents intercepted his letter and thrown it away? Possible, but unlikely. They despised him, but she'd received all his previous notes. So, realistically, he'd been too cocky, too complacent, too overconfident that she'd agree, and now it'd come back to bite him on the bollocks.

His parents had warned him about this exact outcome and he'd ignored their advice. Of course. What did they know about being a teenager ripped from his home and relocated to a foreign country? What did they know about what it truly took to successfully live and love? They cared for each other, but he strove for more than that.

Gabe was fucking nineteen, his own man, right? He made his own decisions, knew what worked for him, what he wanted. He and Tessa had huge plans to open a bar—Lovebirds—overlooking the water.

He'd go to culinary school to give discipline to his love of cooking, and she'd do a business degree in hospitality. And they'd work together, be lifelong partners. A match made in fucking heaven.

As clichéd and cheesy as it sounded, he craved a forever love.

Was that now ripped away from him too?

Gabe didn't want to believe it, but she'd shattered his hopes, sending him straight to purgatory. The hellish spot where he'd stood alone all day, sadly made it real.

He reached the elevator and rode the lift, with a handful of overly cheerful, probably intoxicated party people, his sullen, pathetic, sunburned reflection hitting him hard in the face. He slumped against the cold metal wall and immediately shot forward, the contrasting temperature a shock to his sensitive skin. *Fuck me!*

The elevator doors dinged, opened at his floor, and he traveled down the corridor to his empty Las Vegas hotel room. Once inside, he cranked up the air conditioner and had a cold shower, which did little to wash off the stress and heart-wrenching disappointment of the day.

He should have said he loved her in person, over the phone, in letters. Never should he ever have assumed she knew.

Should he call her and check if she'd gotten his message, check if she was okay? Or would that add additional unwanted pressure? Would it make him sound like a pitiful loser, a total control freak? Would his actions wreak of someone angling for his own way? Most likely she'd see it in that vein … if she'd decided against him.

The dejecting circumstances snuffed out his desire to stay for the remainder of the weekend. He'd looked forward to spending the next couple of days in bed with his new wife and, in between, shopping for their new life together as well as checking out the bars and restaurants. But now, he'd lost all motivation.

His eagerness to further check out Vegas, to pursue his dream to become a chef and work in his own establishment, with his partner in every sense, had been bloody well and truly decimated.

Gabe shut off the water and shivered, goosebumps rising all over his skin. He dried himself, dressed in clean shorts and a t-shirt, grabbed his plane ticket, and changed the return date to early tomorrow.

His parents had always warned him not to fully invest his heart in Tessa, that she wouldn't take him seriously. They'd constantly reinforced that given the time and space, she'd move on to someone else, a man more within her stratosphere. And obviously she had. So now he had to go home and most likely get an earful, a harsh-as-fuck reality check.

SANDRA CARMEL

Chapter Two

San Destino, 21ˢᵗ March 2024

First thing in the morning, Tessa Wren loved strolling through town, doing a circuit from her home in Bloomington to Providence Pier which overlooked Kismet Cove. She'd taken that route almost every day of her adult life. The salty sea air cleared her head and got her off to a fresh mental, emotional, and physical start.

But today, it felt different. Not bad, just … strange. Maybe it had something to do with it falling on the anniversary of Gabe leaving San Destino. Leaving her. Memories of him flooded her mind, more than they had for years.

The sun shone, unblocked by clouds in the bright blue sky, however an unusually swirly breeze had picked up the moment she left the house, whipping her long caramel hair across her face.

Spring was known for its squally conditions, but something in the air suggested a significant change was afoot. Normally, she didn't consider herself superstitious, and blamed her mom, and her mom's New Age friends, for putting the thought into her consciousness, for setting the hard-to-shake foundation.

Tessa shook her head, still not believing her gullibility back then. She'd sat in on a meeting with her mother's spiritual group once, and never again. There'd been too much unfounded, ritualistic crap. Not one of them had shown even a smidge of belief in evidence-based science and the power of a person's choices.

A trolley trundled along the peninsula circuit track, doing its daily loop, already packed with people She loved that it provided an easily accessible option for tourists, older citizens, and the mobility challenged, as well as everyday townsfolk to independently get around key areas of town without needing a car. In recent years, central San Destino had become way too busy, too hard, and expensive to find viable parking spots.

She entered Juniper Hollow and kept walking—a woman on a mission. Sure, universal fate may play a part in what happened to someone, but she believed in people taking responsibility for their actions and inactions. To achieve any success in life, an individual needed to take control, rather than blame others or leave decisions to some unknown, invisible, all-seeing, all-knowing entity.

If she partook in all that shit, she'd be married. If fate and destiny were real, she'd be with Gabe, the indisputable love of her life. Except, instead, she'd lost touch with the guy, and they'd spent the last twenty-one years living separate lives.

A row of shops lined the path, a mishmash of colors like a rainbow lollipop. A sweet, visually appealing spectacle, they matched the cool, busy, fun feel of the area. She'd reach Nina's Bakery soon—the cute, cozy, welcoming spot she and Gabe had frequented almost every day after school.

Why hadn't he sent her the meet-up letter? He'd promised he would, had assured her he wanted them to be together. So, what had happened? Had he changed his mind? Had he met someone else?

Had he fallen victim to dire circumstances? With her failed attempt to chase it up, she'd tried not to think about it too much and, over the years, her thoughts had unsurprisingly dissipated.

Not today. Today everything Gabe, his image, his essence, had bounced around her brain, pressing for acknowledgment, bizarrely heightened after all this time apart.

Granted, when he'd left, they were seventeen and

naive, with rose-colored-glasses securely fixed to their faces, believing anything was possible. Over the next two years, they'd regularly corresponded, sometimes even talked on the phone when her parents weren't home, and he'd sworn he'd send a meet-up date and place soon.

She'd eagerly waited by the mailbox for months to make sure she intercepted the postman and ensure her parents wouldn't confiscate his letter.

But nothing.

Not a word. Not a call, not a note about the proposed in-person catch up.

It took six months before she accepted he wouldn't write. Wouldn't phone. Wouldn't make contact.

A sudden, stronger gust of wind thrust her forward with such force it almost blew her over, so she ducked in closer to the shops. The smell of bacon, eggs, and freshly baked bread made her stomach growl. As soon as she got home, she'd devour some raisin toast—her favorite—with salted butter.

Gabe had gotten her into that, into so many things. She'd especially loved his special Lovebirds omelet, the one he'd created for her, that only he could make to perfection. Only he could hit all the right, satisfying spots.

The toast, however, she could easily emulate. Her taste buds tingled, a shiver of delight shimmying up her spine. Over twenty years had passed, but he had remained alive in her thoughts, particularly on the anniversary of his unforeseen, heartbreaking departure. He'd left his calling card in every cell of her body. So many things still reminded her of the guy who had stolen her heart.

No. No more reminiscing about stuff she couldn't control. She needed to put any unresolved feelings for him to pasture and scrutinize each storefront for job vacancies, having left the last company she'd worked for a couple of weeks ago.

If she had no luck, she'd resort to social media and check out the San Destino community page. She'd rather source something in person, but burned-out beggars couldn't be choosers.

Tessa slowed her pace and waved to her close friend, Lavinia, who worked in the cute, home-style bakery, owned by her Zia Milla, continued past the florist and fish market, and ambled along Providence Pier, past Jack's Bar, and the cool, pink-purple of Bebidas toward a brand-spanking new establishment. The whole town had hardly spoken of anything else.

No one knew the business name or the owner, and it drove the gossip highway crazy. So much for psychic powers. If they existed, wouldn't at least one community member know something?

Fuck. The word rose into her mind like a talisman to Gabe. Every time she thought it, said it, she relived memories of her potty-mouthed teenage sweetheart. Even now. Tragic. So fucking tragic. Why hadn't she moved on? She'd had a shit-ton of opportunities, but nothing and no one had felt as right as him, as right as their union.

Though, how right was he if he'd chosen not to follow through on what he'd promised? She stared out into the choppy blue bay, an indefinable, unsettled energy penetrating her bones. Traffic stopped and started across the bridge, though peak hour would kick in soon, slowing progress to a crawl.

She continued her stroll, past a kaleidoscope of cafes and tourist shops, toward the pinnacle of the pier, where colorful boats bobbed in the water. Gabe would have loved that. Instead of Lovebirds—the business name they'd decided on to reflect their bird-connected surnames, Raven and Wren, the name that reflected the love they shared—he'd probably have changed it to The

Pinnacle.

Mind you, neither one of them had ever straight up said those three vulnerability-inducing words. But they'd both known. No one had ever made love to her like he had. Her bittersweet first time had occurred the last time they'd spent the afternoon together in person.

Her first sexual experience and possibly forever the best. They'd shared so much passion, free from the full confines of adult society, free from responsibility, from insecurity-driven judgment and expectation.

They should have stayed in contact. They should have opened their dream bar. They should have stayed together. So many shoulds...

Once she'd gotten over the hurt of Gabe not sending the meet-up note, she'd tried calling him, but the number was disconnected. She'd written to him as well, and all her letters came back unopened, marked, '*Return to sender, not at this address*'.

At just before 8:00 AM, she reached the end of Providence Pier and swung around to suss out the new, still-to-be-named place. It looked fancy, flashy. She peered in the window, some construction evident inside. A notice farther up advertised for staff and promoted the opening for the following Friday night.

In her eyes, Friday nights would eternally remain special because she and Gabe had claimed them as their own. Due to their parents' work schedules, Fridays allowed them the one time during the week that they could consistently be alone. Until late.

"Excuse me."

She whipped around to find a couple of workmen trying to erect a sign.

"Sorry, ma'am. Please step back. We'll only be a few minutes, if you want to wait."

A sign. *The* sign. The new name. No way would

she go anywhere now. She'd have to hold off a bit longer for her post-walk coffee and raisin toast. In moments, she'd be the talk of the gossipy town, revered for her on-the-pulse provision of information.

An ear-splitting smash almost knocked her backward. Her eyes darted toward the bridge, a car crash stopping traffic, an explosion of letters, and a flurry of flowers fluttering across the bay.

The Free Spirit Bell tolled, just like when the Espiritu Libre ferry crashed in 1949—according to the historical accounts of the incident—the wind picking up into a mini-twister, collecting the envelopes and fresh blooms, and transporting them into town.

A swarm, like biblical locusts, whacked and slapped her body, weirdly not losing momentum. The mail and mix of flowers kept coming and coming, and she shielded her eyes with her forearms, further deflecting the bizarre barrage.

After what seemed like ages, but was probably only a few seconds, maybe a minute, the ferocity eased, and she tentatively lowered her arms, an envelope and two white roses smacking her right in the sternum. She reflexively slammed her hand to her heart, and snatched the letter before it blew away. She went to put it in her bag to repost, when the handwriting stopped her, dead still.

No.

No way.

It couldn't be.

She closed her eyes, rubbed them with the back of her hand, took a deep breath, then scrutinized the script.

Gabe's fucking handwriting.

She stared and stared at her address in his horribly distinctive, hard-to-read cursive. She flipped it over to reveal his old address, the one he'd supposedly left a few months after their last correspondence.

Tessa turned the letter over again and searched for the postmark.

"Oh!" She clutched her chest and stumbled. Dated a week after they'd last spoken. She tore the envelope open and unfolded the note.

My darling Tessa,

How I've missed you. Phone calls and letters are little compensation for us being together in person. But I hope to rectify that soon.

Come away with me. Just you and I. Meet me in Vegas at 1pm on 31st October 2003, in front of the Garden Chapel at the Flamingo, and be my wife. Be mine.

All you need to do is buy your ticket and pack your bag. I'll arrange everything else.

If you don't arrive, I'll assume you've changed your mind about us.

I hope with all my heart to see you soon. I can't wait to share my life with you.

Yours always,

Gabe x

"Oh my God! No!" Tears burst from her eyes, the culmination of pent-up grief pouring out, representing the past twenty-plus years. She could have been with him. They could have been married. They could have had children.

All that time she'd thought he'd changed his mind, but he had entirely fulfilled his promise. And she'd never shown up. He would have believed her non-appearance meant she'd moved on without him. Her lack of presence would have no doubt rammed home her final answer.

But it hadn't, it fucking hadn't. Anguish bombarded her body—her stomach clenched, her eyes burned, her hands fidgeted—the overall anxiety shoving and pummeling and stabbing her with overwhelming helplessness and regret.

She would have said *yes*. No hesitation, no doubt. She would have found a way to get to the safest halfway point between them. She'd have done whatever it required to reach him, to elope, to be his wife.

Sucking gulps of air into her lungs, she folded forward, the letter clasped tightly to her chest—she'd never let go of him again if she had a second chance—devastation circulating right through her system, spreading to the scarred core of her soul.

Why had his letter never been delivered? Had her parents sent it back without her knowing? She'd thought she'd been first to the postman every time, but maybe she hadn't. She couldn't even check with them now. Not that it would benefit them either way anymore.

However, if they had done the unthinkable, thrown such a huge obstacle in her path to prevent her from being with Gabe, whether they believed it was for her best interests or not, was that a forgivable offense?

An obstinate gust of wind blew behind her and she stumbled forward, swiping her hair from her face and glancing up at the newly erected sign above the bar. *Lovebirds.*

"Lovebirds?" She read and reread the word. She blinked, then blinked again. She closed her eyes, and when she opened them, the name hadn't changed.

It had to be a coincidence. Gabe didn't even live in San Destino, hadn't for such a long time. Maybe the liveliness of Lovebirds somehow linked with the nostalgic memories of him that had plagued her this morning more than usual.

Tessa shook her head, trying to clear the reminiscent fog from her brain. She had to think rationally, practically, realistically, not get caught up in memories that no longer formed part of her reality. She refused to get carried away with all that San Destino supernatural stuff.

Focus on facts. She needed a hospitality job and Lovebirds was hiring, and opening soon, according to the advertisement in the window. And it offered the first vacancy she'd seen in an area she wanted to pursue, so she should apply.

Maybe it was a positive omen.

The name alone felt like kismet. How ironic that Providence Pier overlooked Kismet Cove and the broader Starfall Bay. If she'd taken after her mom, she would have read into what the sign might mean, the synchronicity of it all. Sometimes she really wished she could be a believer.

She tucked Gabe's letter carefully into her bag, determined to apply for the duty manager position, but would accept a lesser-paid bartender role, if required. At this stage, she'd do almost anything to return to the industry she loved with the possibility of moving up.

Tessa power walked back along the pier, tempted to jump on the trolley, but decided she needed to dissipate some of her built-up tension and excitement.

As she'd discussed with Gabe back in high school, she'd do a hospitality business course while he pursued cooking. Had he ended up continuing in that direction? She had honored her word, finishing her degree with top marks, and had fallen into a pattern of burying herself in her work. She'd had lots of offers to move to the mainland, to another state, but her gut—or maybe fear—had convinced her to remain in San Destino.

Over the years, she'd enjoyed a stable, not particularly eventful working life, and it had suited her …

maybe too much. But in recent months, she'd gotten twitchy, the career version of a stuck-at-home, travel-lover with itchy feet.

Although she wanted to remain in San Destino long term, she needed something fresh, new, enlivening. Never before had she left a job without anywhere else to go. Possibly an impulsive move, but she'd apply to Lovebirds and see.

If that didn't pan out, she'd re-evaluate. However, her intuition suggested she shouldn't question anything, that she had found the right path. That she needed to go with it, and not be afraid.

In fifteen minutes, she'd returned to her Bloomington home, super windswept, with her mind still a whirlwind of thoughts. *Focus!*

While trying to corral her busy brain, she ate her raison-toast-with-salted-butter breakfast and washed up, then flipped open her compact laptop, reviewed the San Destino community social media page, the Lovebirds 'help required' ad coming to the forefront. She read through the opportunities, adjusted her job application template and CV, and sent it all to Lovebirds.

Now, just like more than twenty years ago, she had to wait on her fate.

Chapter Three

After getting stuck on the bridge, traveling from the airport into San Destino, following some mail truck and car collision, Gabe finally drove into the heart of the city.

Vibrant tiered houses, mansions, and apartment buildings dotted the striking, hilly streets on the way to his cabin near Eden Falls, in Mount Mystique, perched in among the quiet, peaceful, pine-tree-covered mountains. The beauty was overwhelming, just like he remembered.

"Satellite" by Harry Styles played on the radio as he traversed the windy roads. Fuck, he loved that song. Fuck, he loved this place. He had missed it, had missed Tessa terribly. Being back in town ramped up his thoughts of his adolescent sweetheart, the landscape capturing her vibe so accurately.

After she hadn't shown up in Vegas, he'd joined the military instead of culinary school. Initially he'd resisted his parents' wishes but was glad he'd conceded. The armed forces had been good to him.

Beyond good. They'd allowed him to realize his dream. In part. They'd paid for his chef training, and he'd retired on a great pension. Signing up to the US army had provided him a fucking heap of options, had permitted him to pursue his career goals and aspirations.

Would she be proud?

He couldn't complain, well, except when it came to her, and his attempt at romantic relationships since.

Oh, he'd had plenty of sex, but nothing sustainable, nothing long-lasting, nothing that came even close to soulmate stuff. No one had compared to what he'd felt for his first love. He knew he should get over her, gave himself an almost daily pep talk about the importance of cutting the tether to Tessa and moving forward.

Gabe had tried and tried and tried some more, but he couldn't successfully sever the persistent, unbreakable tie between them. Just when he thought he could get over her, a tune, a dish, something, anything would remind him of Tessa. He'd quickly learned that physical chemistry fizzled when it lacked substance, when it lacked the level of connection they'd shared.

The GPS told him to take the next turn, and he began climbing the curvy road to his new home.

His mind immediately reverted to thoughts and images of his beloved teenage Tessa. He'd last seen her in 2001, the night both of them had first had sex. Yet something wouldn't let him shift his focus from her. The woman had etched herself into his heart, making her impossible to forget.

He'd done a fuck-ton of counseling since he returned to civilian life, mostly to do with PTSD, but Tessa kept rearing her beautiful head, and he'd achieved no satisfactory resolution.

He arrived at the rustic log cabin, set among a backdrop of tall, ancient-looking trees and lush green forest. This was the first time he'd seen the property in person.

Buying his home based on the online specs and having it furnished in his absence was a huge risk, but Veronica—the rep from the company he'd used—had consistently received excellent ratings. Viewing the place now reinforced that his initial impression, his gut reaction, had been on the money and had one hundred and fifty percent paid off.

It'd saved him a shit-ton of hours, days, weeks, and exceeded his expectations. It fit right in with the brief he'd provided, fit right in with his style, tastes, and preferences.

Once he'd dumped his bags in the master bedroom, he returned to the living area and dropped onto the plush, cozy-as-fuck couch.

Home.

Somewhere he planned to settle for, well, ever. It was a totally new concept after spending years moving from place to place.

A nomad. First with his family and then with the military. Did he even know what it took, what it required, how it should feel to send down some healthy, grounding roots?

Gabe refocused on his cell phone, the bars barely reaching two. The sketchy reception sucked, but other than that, he loved his new residence, loved the quiet isolation, the *me* time. Fuck, working in a busy kitchen, he needed it, needed a no-people, solo-pursuit space.

It was exactly what had prompted his choice.

No, not just that. As ridiculous as it sounded, he'd hoped to reconnect with Tessa … if she still lived in San Destino and was single. He'd done a preliminary social media search but either she had her settings on private, didn't subscribe, or had gotten married and changed her name, because he couldn't find her.

However, even if he did, and she was serious about another man, he wanted her around in some way, assuming she also agreed. Gabe wasn't greedy or forceful. He'd take whatever he could ethically get, and always, always with her consent.

His phone rang, jolting him out of his reminiscence. *Tessa?* As if. What was he thinking? How would she even know his number? How would she even know he'd come back?

Random, and ridiculously unlikely. And yet, San Destino had magical elements. He'd recognized that from the moment his family moved to the town in his teens. The spirit of the place had drawn him here, formed part of the reason he'd returned.

Gabe stared at the caller ID on the screen. No picture, yet the sequence of figures looked familiar. He answered and put his phone on speaker.

"Gabe?"

"Yes."

"It's Veronica. I wanted to make sure you made it okay, and the cabin meets your expectations."

Oh. Nice of her to check in, but equally, irrationally disappointing. "I did, and it does. You did a great job. Thank you. I just arrived and need to settle in. As soon as I do, I'll contact you if I have any further feedback."

"I'm happy to hear it meets the criteria we discussed, based on first impressions. Please let me know if you need any other assistance."

"I will." Such a lovely, helpful woman. He'd definitely leave a positive review, once he got organized.

A reminder popped onto his phone screen about all the shit he needed to complete prior to the grand opening of Lovebirds—his passion project. Scheduled for the 29th of March, the eve of the Easter weekend, just over a week away, he still had a lot to do, like hire most of the required staff. Much to his amazement, no worries wore away at his usually agitated, hypersensitive nerves.

Everything else, business and relocation-wise, had gone to plan, so far. Everything else had clicked into place as though driven by destiny. Kind of freaky, yet equally not surprising, given the town's name and feel.

Fuck, he'd only spent a short time in the region, but it'd been the best few years of his young life. The highlight of his life full stop. Essentially, San Destino had inspired his career decisions, had drawn him to Tessa.

San Destino had set him up to meet his soulmate. Back then, anyway.

Would he run into her? He had everything fucking crossed. He wanted to see Tessa, talk to her, give her a well overdue hug. Hold on to her, however he could.

How did she look? How would she respond to him? Had what they'd shared held a place in her heart? It certainly had for him. Was she still as sweet? Had she married? Did she have children? Whatever her situation, he fucking hoped she was happy. That's all he ever wanted for her and himself, whether they were apart or together. Preferably together.

Gabe closed his eyes, relaxed against the backrest, and his fucking phone rang. Again. He blew out a frustrated breath—it was way past knock-off time—but, with a new business opening up sooner than soon, and being right slap-bang in Tessa territory, he answered. "Gabe here."

"Sorry to ring out of hours but just wanted to confirm interview times for next week. If the applicants are as impressive as their CVs, the opening is going to be a huge success."

Lewis. His reliable, very enthusiastic, perfectionistic PA-come-acting-bar manager.

And he'd offered unexpected but welcome news. Who'd have thought such a small town could produce so much potential talent? But then again, it had produced Tessa and so far, no one had come close to comparable.

"Good to hear. Complete the shortlist then book the interviews for Monday at Lovebirds. My office should be sorted by then. Fingers crossed we'll discover some gems so we can get on with the rest of the pre-opening shit."

"Yes! If there are any issues, I'll let you know."

They hung up and Gabe plugged his phone in to

charge beside him. Even the outlets were well appointed. Clear, convenient, practical. Just how he liked his kitchens.

He thrust his hands behind his head and got comfy. From the moment he'd bought the bar, everything had fallen into place. His cost-effective, perfect cabin had pretty much dropped into his lap, plus he'd found cheap flights, with a bonus, first-class upgrade, and had finally ditched his clingy, gold-digger girlfriend.

Fucking unbelievable how free and on-track he felt, and all from putting fear aside and making positive changes, cutting loose the last of his heavy emotional baggage. The seamless flow indicated he'd made the right move. Or so he hoped.

When launching a new business, starting anything from a fresh standpoint, no one could ever be sure. The town was steeped in a broad range of cultures, traditions, and massive superstition.

Would they welcome a blow-in like him, a guy who'd arrived in his teens and barely created a blip in the community before having to leave? Could he attract the clientele he required, could he fit within the current climate and beliefs? The entrenched citizens would most likely say he'd only lived in San Destino for five minutes, in the scheme of things ... assuming they even remembered him.

If they did, could they accept him into the cliquey fold? Yes, he could potentially appeal to a younger audience, but to increase his chances of overall acceptance and sustainability, he really needed a stalwart of the region to back him and his vision. But who?

These days he didn't know anyone, except Veronica, and they'd only ever emailed, spoken on the phone occasionally, and had the odd video call. Maybe he should contact local radio stations for an interview, post a

Lovebirds opening ad on the town's social media page, and possibly do a live promo clip?

He grabbed his phone and did another search for Tessa on socials. Outside of wanting to reconnect on a personal level, she'd be a great ambassador for Lovebirds.

Nothing.

Dammit.

Next step, he'd do some networking and subtle investigation with local businesses, once he'd better established himself.

The gorgeous girl appeared in vivid, full-color detail in his mind, clear as the last day he'd seen her. A sentimental smile tugged at his lips.

He'd had four fantastic years with her, the longest he'd lived anywhere, and just when he'd set down some solid roots, his parents had yanked him away. Again. He should have been used to it, de-fucking-sensitized, but he fucking wasn't.

He'd begged and pleaded to stay, but being underage, they'd refused. And he'd had no recourse. If her parents had liked him, he could have sought their support, but...

Gabe sat forward, scrubbed his hands hard over his face, and sighed. Nothing and no one, before or since leaving Tessa, had broken his heart like she had. Not to that extent. Sadness, yeah, he'd experienced episodes, but usually they resolved after a short while.

Not in this case. Not when it came to Tessa. If only he knew why she'd decided against him. Except he may never know, had to learn to accept it, learn how to deal with the lack of closure.

Even with her rejection, her essence, her energy had continued to burn like inextinguishable embers in his heart, simmering away in the background, never too far from the forefront of his mind. Gabe craved her like a hot, hearty, slow-cooked stew—tempting, irresistible, restorative. Unforgettable.

So many small things reminded him of her—songs, phrases, food, landmarks—especially now he'd returned to Tessa-town.

Flicking through his phone, Gabe stopped on the last photo he'd taken of them. Yeah, he was that tragic guy who held on to the girlfriend that got away and ensured he transferred her pic onto every new upgraded device.

The heat of her body crushed against his came flashing back as though it had happened weeks, not years, ago. Their faces virtually squished together, his soft, virgin stubble scraping against her smooth skin, their smiles so broad they just about extended off the screen. Her silky caramel-blonde hair cascaded over his shoulder, her exceptional hazel eyes clear and bright and enticing. Full of promise.

Did she ever think about him? Or had she stopped the day she decided they shouldn't elope? Even though she'd chosen not to meet him in Vegas, he still cared, a piece of her lodging deep in his heart.

He thought about her way too fucking much, way too fondly. Nostalgia tended to do that, make a person remember the good times. And they'd had plenty, shared plenty together. He wished they still could.

A sudden desire for her signature dish, the dish she'd inspired, the dish he'd made for her all those years ago, popped into his head. He had to do it for dinner. Maybe it would call to their combined dynamism, conjure her presence, somehow deliver her back into his life.

The fucking out-there, far-fetched idea appealed more than it should. And he hadn't even been drinking.

Since when did he believe in all the San Destino superstitious hocus-pocus stuff?

Since it connected him to Tessa. He'd experienced similar mystical beliefs in his Celtic heritage, but he'd left them behind when he came to America. Without Tessa, they didn't resonate.

San Destino locals generally kept quiet about their unconventional faith, but ask the right questions and they professed to have a subsection of their population with magical powers. He found it fascinating, and wished it'd bring him his coveted outcome, but he refused to rely on hope.

He subscribed to having the power of choice. All he could do was control his own decisions in order to put himself in the most suitable places and make the most of any opportunities.

Were some things out of people's control? Fuck yes. But so many decisions came down to state of mind combined with environmental circumstances. And those choices influenced final results. Fuck, he wouldn't be in his current affluent position if he hadn't chosen well.

On the romance side of things, not so much. He'd never been an expert in that area; however, Tessa had. She'd taught him heaps, taught him that food played a part in attraction, pleasure.

Over and over, she'd shown him that it had aphrodisiac properties, some selections and combinations more than others. She'd reinforced the saying that *the way to a person's heart was through their stomach*, had some merit.

It helped that he fucking loved cooking. Had loved her. Still did. The two constant loves in his life. At this point, it didn't matter if she reciprocated. He just wanted her around in his small sphere of existence.

Without question, he'd been in lust since her, but

nothing more. Had she felt that level of connection too? Or had she found love with another man?

When his bar opened this coming week, if she still lived in town, would she check it out? Was that her thing? Would she be curious, hold the same compulsive eagerness to see him? Would she wonder whether he was behind Lovebirds? A real-life remnant from their teenage legacy.

Would she regret her decision not to meet him in Vegas? Or had fate dictated the best path for each of them? Soon they'd both turn forty. Fuck. Where had the years gone?

He strode into the cabin's refitted, contemporary kitchen, ready to start dinner. Cooking with wonderful equipment in a great setting had always given him joy, focus, motivation, and a much-needed distraction from everyday stresses ... provided he had a balance between repetitive, hands-on work and creativity. He had to factor in time on his own to study, evaluate, and innovate.

As he'd requested, his pantry and cupboards had been stocked with quality food, pots, pans, cooking utensils, dishes and cutlery, and from what he could see, the required cleaning products.

He started on his Lovebirds omelet—quick, simple, and nourishing, as well as an ode to Tessa, and an alignment with the Spanish-influenced history of the town. Without fucking toasted bread as a side. He'd never understood that western society addition.

Toast and an omelet, in his opinion, didn't go together. If he wanted carbs he'd add grated potato to the mix, or a side of legumes, preferably baked beans. It harked back to his Scottish cooked-breakfast heritage. Out of everywhere he'd ever visited, they did the best, heartiest fry-up.

Keeping with the exact replication of the dish, he

arranged it on the plate, using his beloved cutters to form the shape of two birds—Wren and Raven—beak-to-beak, kissing. What he'd envisaged for their partnership privately, professionally. It had determined, solidified, decided the name of the business they'd created together. The name reflected them entirely.

Lovebirds. What he'd pictured, strove for, had finally become a reality, from a professional perspective, anyway. Half realized was better than never realized at all, right?

Having hardly eaten during the day, he scarfed down his dinner. Tasty, nutritious, and fucking delicious. Just like Tessa. Plus, he'd packed the meal full of superfoods—tomato, silverbeet, broccoli, and avocado, and added a bit of onion, cheese, and tuna—to temporarily feed his unsatiated emotional hunger. He had to add his teenage concoction to the all-day-breakfast menu.

Gabe made a note on his phone, washed up, and had a quick shower.

San Destino had retained its historic aspects, and warm, friendly large country-town feel, while also changing, progressing, and expanding. It still had a good, welcoming, supportive vibe overall. A vibe he wanted to continue to foster.

He walked to the window, a towel tucked around his waist, and stared at the twinkling lights brightening the township. So fucking pretty. As pretty as the woman who'd stolen his heart. No, the lights and view were secondary. Even the amazing starlight couldn't compare.

Maybe his memory of Tessa had built up her magic in his mind? Back then, he was a fucking horny teenager. Maybe he'd over-inflated her impact. Maybe she'd changed now. Twenty-plus years on, they'd both have matured. But maturity didn't necessarily mean he'd outgrown her.

Gabe pressed his palm to the glass, as though to tap into the heartbeat of the town. A reconnection to his lost love. His return hinged on living out the dream he'd discussed in depth with his childhood sweetheart. Well, part of the dream. The part that didn't include her. Sadly. Regrettably. But it had been her choice. Right?

A shooting star arced across the sky, leaving a trail of glowing, sparkly stardust.

Bring Tessa back to me.

There, he'd made his wish. Now he just had to impatiently wait and see if the universe obliged.

Did he need her in order to be successful?

No.

Did he want her in his life?

Yes.

Or at least the chance to re-evaluate whether their connection had withstood the test of their time apart. Had his teenage self, his gut, his intuition gotten it right?

Gabe pushed away from the glass, brushed his teeth, discarded his towel, and got into bed. He lay on his back, his arms folded behind his head, his body vibrating with banked-up, unexpended energy. Energy he desperately wanted to expend on Tessa.

His cock tented the quilt. *Down boy.* "If you're lucky, you might get another go," he said, and chuckled. A longer-lasting encounter would be brilliant. *You know, something like forever, this time.*

He turned onto his side, his thoughts drifting to the upcoming opening, and what inspired his love of the culinary arts. Over the years he'd learned he could make fantastic food for customers, but in his personal life, if he didn't have someone special to cook for, to share his dining innovations with, he lost his motivation, and the process lost its appeal. He lost his cooking mojo.

Gabe regularly sought feedback to ensure his gastronomic skills had hit the required spot. And when he'd gone too fancy, he'd gotten canned, and took the constructive criticism onboard, creating a more user-friendly menu.

Relatable, flavorsome, often comfort food, won customers over. The reminder served him well, ensuring he didn't purely focus on a self-absorbed vision. Getting too caught up in gourmet shit stroked his ego, but went against his desire to attract a broad range of pleased patrons.

He adjusted his position, straightened out the top sheet and realigned the bedspread. Not even a shaft of light penetrated the room. The beauty of blackout blinds. Gabe closed his eyes and tried to wind down, but thoughts swirled around and around and around, jumping from one idea to the next tangential connection in his overactive brain.

Was his opinion skewed? Possibly? Probably. But whose wasn't? That created the foundation of a person's reality. That's where it helped to have someone trusted and loved and cherished to provide constructive criticism. That's where Tessa could assist him to keep in check, accountable, exactly as she'd shown back when they were together.

His beliefs, insecurities, and awareness dictated his thinking. And would persist, as they did with everyone, unless challenged. Like with anything, perspective was key. Stepping away, attempting to switch off emotional biases, and remaining as neutral and grounded as possible, as well as obtaining and weighing up others' thoughts, all played a part in making more positive, successful decisions.

Fuck, if he hadn't applied those principles, he wouldn't have made it back to the US alive.

SANDRA CARMEL

Chapter Four

Monday morning came around quickly. Tessa stood in her hot pink satin dressing gown and dried her hair in front of the bathroom mirror, tingles of anticipation fluttering in her stomach like a swarm of over-eager butterflies.

She hadn't told anyone about the Lovebirds interview, despite having a good feeling flowing through her veins. Better not to tempt fate. Who knew the quality of the other duty manager applications?

She'd only ever managed small restaurants and cafes in San Destino, whereas she might be competing with high caliber candidates from the mainland, who'd worked in Michelin-starred establishments.

What she lacked in high-end experience, she'd make up for in passion. She loved the hospitality industry, loved San Destino, and took pride in her work, making sure patrons had a great time.

From what she'd witnessed, that attitude encouraged loyal, repeat customers to tell their friends and family about their awesome experience. Word of mouth remained one of the best forms of promotion.

Tessa spent the remainder of her morning reviewing her wardrobe in an attempt to find suitable attire for her interview. Instinct convinced her to pick an outfit Gabe would have *fancied*, as he would say—a long flowing skirt and floral top. But rationally it made no sense, given he hadn't been around for ages, given he wouldn't see or appreciate what she'd chosen.

In the past, he'd preferred a lot of cleavage, but that wasn't exactly appropriate for a job interview, so she toned it down. Tessa slipped into some wedge-style sandals, checked her makeup in the dressing-table mirror, and gave herself a mini motivational chat.

You can do this. You're more than qualified, more than capable. You have a passion for working with people. And Lovebirds ... it has to mean something.

She grabbed a light shawl, shoved it in her handbag, and strolled into town.

With a soft breeze and sunny blue skies, it not only felt like the beginning of spring, but also the start of something fresh, exciting, and new.

Twenty minutes later, she reached the pier and tried avoiding the spurts of sea mist attempting to spritz her face, glad she'd decided not to straighten her hair.

Lovebirds loomed ahead, and her nerves jangled like a peal of belligerent bells. She slowed her pace, stopped at the front entrance, and said a silent prayer, even though she didn't believe in all that religious stuff.

Please, universe, let this go well, set me on the right path. She took a deep, calming breath and stepped inside. She needed this job, and wished to somehow, some way, see Gabe.

With so many large windows, the place attracted light, creating an inviting, relaxed atmosphere. The cool blue, white, and beige bar reminded her of a beach holiday resort—beautiful, comfortable, and serene. Whether she got the job or not, she couldn't wait to try the food and service, and see if it matched the high-quality yet accessible, relatable feel.

A young mid-twenties man—groomed to a tee, his hair styled perfectly with just the right amount of product, and dressed in a suit that looked like it cost more than his monthly rent—met her in the center of the main dining room with a big, broad smile, arm outstretched in greeting. "Tessa? I'm Lewis. Welcome to Lovebirds."

"Thank you." She smiled back and shook his hand, equally excited yet disappointed the guy wasn't

Gabe. "It's a spectacular venue. It really makes the most of its positioning." The bay, multi-colored boats, shops, homes, and scenic mountains surrounded Lovebirds, all adding to the allure of the stunning spot.

"It is. It does." His smile morphed into a super-pleased grin. "Follow me and we'll get started."

He led her into a grand office beside a magnificent meeting room and gestured for her to take a seat. "The owner will be joining us shortly."

The head honcho? She sat and tried to keep her hands still, and her feet and legs from shaking. She hadn't expected to meet the man, or woman, until the bar had hired all their staff. But obviously Lovebirds had a hands-on, involved employer. Depending on the person's personality, that could be a pro or a con. A fine line existed between keen interest and micro-management.

Lewis grabbed a computer tablet off the desk and positioned himself opposite. "Let me check a few details while we wait."

He ran through her name and contact info, work history, and references, typing any additional notes. "So, tell me, what brought you to Lovebirds?"

Where did she start? Did she dare speak the full truth? "Honestly, I walked past last week, saw the ad in the window, and on the San Destino socials page, and knew I needed to apply.

"The business name, the position, everything about the place took me back to my late teens. My then-boyfriend and I spoke about a venue exactly like this. We were going to call it Lovebirds—"

"Tessa?"

Gabe's voice.

She froze, temporarily catatonic, her mind and body unable to compute. It couldn't be him. Her heart almost stopped beating. A second passed, two, three, five, ten, and she finally roused enough to turn around.

The man himself stood in the doorway, taller, more filled out, more wrinkled and weathered, more rugged and manly, but just as attractive. He leaned against the doorjamb in jeans and a torso-hugging black t-shirt, his hands fidgety. His nervous tell.

Yet he oozed his characteristic magnetism, virility, and sexiness. "Gabe?"

His midnight blue eyes peered into hers, and he raked a hand through his ever-messy, untamable blond hair. "It *is* you." He strode over and lifted her out of her seat, wrapping her in a full body hug and totally breaching any sort of protocol.

So unexpected in every aspect, especially given she'd stood him up back then. As far as he knew. He'd have assumed she didn't care. But she had, so very much. Maybe the years apart created a certain healing, a certain acceptance, a focus on the positive past, separate from their new future. How could she prove she'd never received the letter, convince him she'd have come if she'd known of his proposal?

He settled her into standing just as quickly as he'd whipped her out of her chair. And she immediately felt the loss of his familiar heat. "Sorry. I just... I can't believe it. My Tessa is right here."

My Tessa. Wow. Possessive, in a good way. A great way. As though he'd experienced the exact same intensity of feeling. Could that be possible? Had he forgiven her for slighting him, or was his show of affection an appreciation of their history, of nostalgia?

Or was it strategic? Had he hoped that getting in good with a local would provide positive promotion for Lovebirds? Had he hoped it'd help give a giant leg-up to his new bar?

No. He wasn't shallow. He'd always been upfront

to the point of blunt, never showing a hint of bullshit, not even to win over her parents. He'd never faked anything, never boasted about himself—left others to comment on his merits—so why would he start talking shit now? Unless he'd experienced things in life that overhauled, reset, and recreated his total character. And not for the best.

"So, this is *your* place?" Where had he been? Had he followed his father into the military, or had he pursued his cooking career? What had he chosen when his teenage sweetheart seemingly rejected him?

"Yeah." He glanced at her with a regretful, it-should-have-been-ours look. It didn't make sense. According to her no-show, all those years ago, she'd chosen to move on. Without him. So why would he worry about excluding her from Lovebirds? He didn't owe her anything.

In line with the spring season, hopefully they, too, could start anew. "It's even better than I imagined."

"Thank you." His poignant smile held a hint of pride and satisfaction.

"So, you and Tessa…?" Lewis stared at his boss and waved his hand between her and Gabe.

"We knew each other a long time ago." Gabe glanced at her with what looked like hesitation, hope. "Do you still want the job?"

"Yes." She didn't even have to think about her response.

"Then you're hired. Orientation is Wednesday at ten, then Thursday I'd like staff to have a trial run and help finish getting everything set up in preparation for the opening on Friday."

"Great. Thank you."

"Thank *you*." He smiled, and left her alone again with Lewis.

Disappointment flooded her heart. She'd expected him to hang around and speak to her some more. Or at least suggest they catch up afterward to give them an opportunity to discuss what had happened. She desperately wanted a chance to explain why she hadn't responded to his letter, why she hadn't made an appearance, and to discuss where to go from here.

What had he done in the meantime? How had his life panned out? Was he happy? If he was single, did he have children? Whether he had a family or not, opening a new business, no doubt, meant he was incredibly busy.

Too busy to prioritize a conversation with a woman who'd abandoned him when it mattered. And she couldn't blame the guy. If their positions were reversed, if not angry, she'd have harbored massive disillusionment.

Her ego would have taken a huge hit, whatever trust they'd established broken, damaged. Almost impossible to piece back together. Except he'd been welcoming, his elevated level of emotional maturity adding to his sexiness.

Given this new, unexpected eventuation, she assumed she'd see him regularly. At least she hoped she would. But maybe once he'd hired all the required staff, he'd step back and be a hands-off owner? Leave again. Disappear from her life.

No, he loved cooking too much. He'd have some physical presence, to ensure his standards were met. So she could try and slot in a time for them to have a decent chat. Assuming he wanted to. Assuming he had the fortitude to foster some sort of positive relationship, and not detour down an unhelpful path.

If nothing else, she wanted closure. He probably did too. And if so, maybe she could finally move forward. So much time had passed between them, a few more days or weeks wouldn't matter. Would it? As long as they had an opportunity to seek out a resolution, to set their new situation straight.

"Congratulations! I look forward to working with you." Lewis's voice jolted her mind back to the present.

"Thanks. Same. Ah … what's the salary?" she blurted, still trying to get her head around seeing Gabe and what that might mean.

"Above the current award. I'll send you everything in writing so you can have a look and compare it against industry standards."

"Sounds good. I appreciate it." She'd gone into automatic-pilot mode, still not quite believing Gabe had returned to San Destino. "All being well, I'll see you Wednesday. Any particular dress code, uniform?"

"Whites, beiges, blues. It's all in the orientation pack." It matched perfectly with the Lovebirds color scheme. He grabbed a folder off the desk and handed it to her. "I'll also email you a copy and include your digi-sign contract. Any questions, let me know."

"I will. Thanks." She exited the office and scoured the surroundings as subtly as possible, searching for Gabe. But she couldn't see him anywhere. Part of her floated on fluffy cloud nine at the successful job interview outcome, and part of her sank into sadness at his disappearance.

To offer her the position, he obviously wanted her present, still a somewhat key part of Lovebirds. But was it out of caring, her suitability for the role, or guilt-infused obligation? She didn't know which answer she preferred.

Tessa started the brisk walk back to her house, her mind buzzing. She wanted him to give them a chance at a possible reunion, but not hire her as the duty manager if she wasn't the best candidate. She didn't want or need a favor. Her skills, passion, and personality would get her the right job. Eventually.

Not even a minute after she stepped inside her front door, her cell phone rang. *Unknown number* flashed onto the screen, which she normally declined, but her gut compelled her to answer. It could be Lovebirds. "Hello?"

"Tessa, it's Gabe." His voice still had remnants of that deep, distinctive Scottish lilt further enhanced on the phone for some reason.

She sank onto the couch. "Hi."

"I didn't see you leave."

"I didn't see you when I left."

He laughed, exactly as she remembered, as irresistible as ever. "Touché. It was a lovely surprise, having you so close, in person. After so long."

"You too. You look good. Well. Are you happy?"

"Very."

Did he mean professionally, personally, both? "I imagine it's pretty amazing finally opening Lovebirds."

"It is. Not exactly how I'd envisioned it, but I'm grateful."

So was she. "Do you live locally?"

"Just moved into a place in Mount Mystique, near Eden Falls. You?"

"Still in my parents' place—"

"That cute little white and pink house in Bloomington?"

"Good memory. That's the one." With Gabe's parents often working late and her family disapproving of him, they'd spent most of their free time at his home. "Unfortunately, Mom and Dad are both gone now."

"Sorry to hear that."

Was he? They'd made things extremely hard for him, hard for them as a couple. Maybe he thought they'd had a part in her not appearing back then? She still questioned it herself. Not that she, or anyone, would ever know for certain. "Thanks."

"We should meet up. Outside of work. How about after orientation on Wednesday?"

Oh. Part of her wanted to know exactly where he'd lived during the intervening years, what he'd been up to, how he'd changed, how much of him was still the same, if he had kids, a live-in partner, a wife. And part of her feared his answers and what they'd mean for her going forward. Not that she and Gabe could necessarily rekindle what they'd had, even if he was single, but still... "Okay."

"Stay at the bar and have a drink or two, on the house, and I'll come and find you. Or you can come and find me."

"I look forward to it." This time, she didn't hold back her honest thoughts. If her eagerness and curiosity to catch up with him was a turn off, that already said a lot.

"Me too. You know that, yes." His voice had dropped into that warm, smooth, sensual tone, like delectable, melted chocolate.

They both hesitated.

"See you Wednesday." They hung up, and she put her phone on to charge. Then she went to have a shower, taking her Gabe-sized, waterproof vibrator with her. For years, she'd fantasized about surprising him with the simple yet powerful device, and putting on a little self-pleasure show.

In the short time they'd spent together as a couple, he'd loved watching her get off, whether he brought her to climax or she did it herself with her own hand. But she'd never gotten the chance to do a private demo with her preferred buzzy friend, and had chosen to only ever use her number-one sex toy on her own.

It hadn't felt right introducing her Gabe-inspired vibrator to any other man. Just the thought had betrayal burning in her stomach like severe acid reflux, even though they were no longer together. She'd changed batteries numerous times during their period apart, but other than that, the device kept going and going, as strong as ever. A bit like her feelings for him.

Once the water reached the right heat level, she stepped underneath the spray, closed her eyes, flicked on the switch of her solo substitute lover, then dragged it over her breasts and slowly down between her legs. She pressed the head to her clit, sending wave upon wave of vibrating goodness to her core, and bucked into it, wanting more.

Repositioning the toy at her entrance, she thrust onto it, taking the faux phallus deep, and adjusted the vibration to the highest intensity. With one hand, she fucked herself with her buzzy buddy, and with her free fingers, she played with her breast and tweaked her nipple, imagining the current Gabe taking her to ecstasy.

In seconds, he did, well, the imaginary version did. She came hard, the orgasm so forceful she braced her hand against the tiles and cried out, the hot water beating down on her, her moans echoing around the room, obliterating the hum of his proxy penis.

Fuck, it was good. Not as good as having his hot-blooded hands, body, mouth, and member. But still superb. Considering the years that had passed, and their relationship experience, no doubt they'd both be better lovers. However, that all came down to whether they'd had the inclination to go there, the interest, the freedom.

And if they did, skill and expertise played a part in enhancing pleasure but couldn't take the place of passion. No one could fake that invisible but potent ingredient.

She switched off her substitute buddy-with-benefits, cleaned and rinsed him under the steady stream of water, and proceeded to wash herself thoroughly. Two more days until she'd see the real Gabe again. Would he phone her in between? Text her?

He hadn't given her his private number, so she couldn't call or message him directly, which was probably a good thing. Technically, she'd agreed to be an employee, not his sweetheart. Not even his hook-up.

Getting involved with workers produced a potential conflict of interest. What was his stance on that? What was hers? It definitely could add more complications to the work environment.

Whether things went well or not, other employees may assess her as receiving special biased treatment, which could create a divisive, unfair, 'favorites' culture. And that reinforced the opposite of a productive, supportive, well-functioning team.

She had to show caution and not partake in behavior that suggested higher privileges. Frequenting the pier on her time off, even if it fell within a section of her regular morning walking route, might seem suss.

Especially if other staff often saw her talking in an overly familiar manner with the boss. So she needed to change up the location of her exercise routine until the staff realized she wasn't a threat, wasn't someone angling for extra benefits.

She expected to work as hard as anyone else. Harder, because she wanted Gabe to do well, be successful, independent of herself. He deserved the best.

She dried her body, threw on a sweatsuit, and packed her vibrator away in her bedside drawer.

How could she possibly concentrate now? Excitement welled up inside her like a balloon ready to pop. She desperately wanted to confide in someone but worried about jinxing the situation.

Ugh. Her mom, and some of her mom's 'spiritual' friends, had really done an annoying number on her. They'd indoctrinated Tessa on a subconscious level. She didn't want to believe in all the San Destino superstitious psychic stuff they'd spouted, but suddenly she couldn't ignore it.

If unable to accept their otherworld idealism wholeheartedly, could she at least tolerate the possibility? Given the circumstances, it didn't make sense for her to risk any obstacle, perceived or otherwise, preventing her and Gabe from a possible second chance.

Chapter Five

Fuck. Tessa.

Right now, if he had the opportunity.

Gabe slumped into his office chair at Lovebirds, her distinctive come-fuck-me perfume still lingering in the room following her interview, bringing back every intimate moment they'd shared.

He sank his hands into his hair. She was just as beautiful, just as pure and angelic as he'd remembered, with that underlying hint of mischief. That contradictory, yet incredibly attractive draw card played right into his desires. Always had. Probably always would.

No. She was sweeter, more breathtaking, if that was even possible. Now she'd become significantly more dangerous to his heart. Everything about her spoke to him on a soul-deep level, even following such a short interaction after all these years. He sat up straight against the back of his seat, sucking in a reality-check breath.

He shouldn't get too carried away. She'd rejected his proposal in the past and could potentially be in a loving, reciprocal, long-term relationship with some other guy. His teeth involuntarily clacked together.

She might see Gabe purely as a pleasant memory. And now she worked for him. Fuck. He had to tread carefully. He didn't want Tessa, or anyone else, thinking he'd employed her with a personal agenda.

Yes, he wanted her happy and within his sphere of existence, but ultimately, he'd hired her because of her previous passion and love of hospitality. Afterward, he'd reviewed her extensive CV and read over Lewis's positive written feedback, determining he'd made the right choice. She was the most qualified person for the position.

Guilt ballooned in his heart. And yeah, okay, he felt bad about pursuing their shared dream, solo.

A knock sounded on Gabe's door.

"Do you have a minute?" Lewis entered his office without waiting for a reply. "Everything all right?"

Gabe couldn't stop the grin from bursting onto his face. "More than all right." Because no matter what, she'd come back into his life.

"She's very beautiful."

And smart and sexy. "Tessa? Yeah, she is. But that's not why I appointed her to the position."

"I know. You're too professional for that."

He was. But now he questioned his decision. Having her working for his business made it difficult for him to make a move. He hadn't thought it through. He'd seen her and wanted to make sure he continued to regularly, however he could.

"Thanks. So, what can I help you with?"

"Nothing. Just checking in. I've finished all the allocated tasks for today. Is there anything else you need done before I leave?"

"No. But thanks for asking. I appreciate you reviewing the job applications, as well as organizing and running the interviews. Your input has been invaluable."

"It's my job. But I'm glad to hear I'm meeting your standards."

His high standards, which he had a reputation for. Gabe's gruff, straight-up attitude polarized people, but his business history showed he'd retained the right staff. It worked to his advantage.

"You are. Now head home."

Gabe strove for the best and that required employees who shared his ideals, his vision. It required him to work with them in a supportive way that maximized their assets and increased productivity.

Tessa had totally subscribed to that. She'd shown the perfect business partner traits, had demonstrated the ideal employee attributes. She'd been his biggest inspiration. Did she still subscribe to the same thinking or had her worldview changed? He'd know soon enough. Wednesday, if he was a lucky bastard.

Now he had to stop focusing on his lady distraction and fixate on the finishing touches of Lovebirds, the final internal fine-tuning before the official opening on Friday. However, with Tessa taking up every single spare brain cell, it made it almost impossible.

Fuck. He'd managed for fucking years without her. He could do it again for a few more days. Couldn't he? He thrust himself out of his chair and checked through the state-of-the-art kitchen, for the hundredth time, then scrutinized the bar's interior.

Awesome. Impeccable. He had the best fucking team, had used the best consultants. Everything was on track, under control. So what the fuck was he supposed to do with himself until he saw Tessa again?

If no issues presented in the interim, he'd come in Tuesday, recheck everything, do a trip to the Hazelwood fresh food market to make sure the orders were sorted and verify delivery of the produce. He would also ensure his sous chef and cooking team had no other questions.

Anything to redirect his attention away from Tessa. He needed patience. Not his forte when it came to her. Normally, he was disciplined as all fuck. Though, by the looks of things, Tessa was and would always be the exception.

The rest of the afternoon Gabe made calls to local suppliers to confirm contracts, and had the few remaining tradesmen on site, completing the final touches to the interior. He stood in the front doorway and did one last slow, scrutinizing walk through.

The construction company had done an amazing job. They had delivered a fucking brilliant end product, which translated to his bar looking top notch. The result one hundred percent replicated his design. What he'd imagined had literally come to life.

Whites and blues mixed with light-colored timber created the beachy color palette and fit right in with the top end of the pier, overlooking the ocean. During the day, it'd maximize the sunshine, and at night, the starlight.

In the large beer garden, he'd fit a web of sparkling fairy lights and a sprinkling of heaters to cater to the cooler weather. In case of rain, he'd installed a retractable clear ceiling, and roll-down walls, to enable year-round use of the area and constant views of the sky and seascape.

He itched to officially open the doors and see if the locals and visitors connected with his vision. Had he gotten it right?

When the last of the workers left, he locked up and drove home, mentally, physically, and emotionally exhausted.

Before crashing into bed, he stood in the kitchen and dug into some leftovers for dinner, then jumped in the shower. Barely able to remain standing, he'd planned for a quick wash, but the hot water cascading over his tired, weary muscles and aching bones soothed and reinvigorated.

Tessa, sitting in his office in that elegant flowy skirt and figure-enhancing floral top, popped into his thoughts. She'd been lovely, professional, and enchanting. She epitomized the look he wanted for his bar, and himself. Fuck, she'd matured into such a stunning woman and oozed bucket loads of sensuality.

And her curves. *Fuck me.* So feminine, so sexy, so sensuous. Without even trying. Back then, she'd had a sweet, seductive shape, but now, her deliciously fuller breasts and cock-stirringly rounded hips had his dick rising to the occasion.

Gabe closed his eyes and focused on Tessa's every detail, carved into his memory. His hand had a mind of its own and grasped his cock. It moved from a slow and steady glide to a fast and firm pump. And fuck, it felt good—great—imagining sinking into her sultry, slick heat.

Every explicit detail bombarded his brain and he thrust faster, harder, furiously collecting pre-cum onto his palm and sliding it over his dick. He called out her name and came, spurting all over his hand, all over the tiles.

"Fuck." He slapped a hand against the wall, breathing hard. In the past eighteen months, he'd been so busy with the Lovebirds project he'd had no time to meet women, let alone go on a date. He needed a good fuck. Preferably with Tessa.

It'd been … shit—over three years since he'd last had sex. He shook his head and stood up straight, now that the strength had returned to his legs. Gabe grabbed the handheld shower and washed the cum-spattered tiles, then himself.

After vigorously drying his body and hair with a bath towel, he entered his bedroom naked. He slipped between the crisp, cool sheets, wishing he could slip into Tessa's moist wet core.

How he'd love her beneath him, in his bed right now. Pleasuring her beautiful body would be his ultimate wish come true. He'd take his time, rediscovering every inch of her skin, every special spot that made her moan.

Like the first time he'd licked her sweet pussy. His first go at oral had happened in his bedroom, at his parents' place straight after school, before his mum and dad returned from work, before he'd told Tessa he'd be leaving.

They'd been making out and he'd slid his fingers into her panties and rubbed her silky wetness. Desire and curiosity had him instructing her to lie back while he whipped off her knickers. He'd pressed her lithe, athletic legs apart and dove down.

She'd gripped his head tightly and bucked up into his face, her little desperate cries filling the room, encouraging his efforts and guiding him forward. It took her less than a minute to come all over his face. It'd been such a turn on tasting her, smelling her arousal, seeing her give in to pleasure. Particularly, pleasure he'd given her.

She'd wanted to return the favor—as she had at the drive-in the week before, and it had been fucking amazing—but they'd ended up stripping off the rest of their clothes and losing their virginity to each other instead, climaxing mere minutes before his parents arrived home. They'd scrambled to get dressed, threw open the window, and tried to wipe the post-sex flush from their faces. If his parents suspected anything, they'd never said.

Did Tessa remember it as fondly as he did? Had he put her on an unrealistic pedestal? Had she decided against him for a reason back then that still translated to now? When they caught up this Wednesday, would she reveal what had made her decide not to choose him, choose them?

Chapter Six

On Wednesday morning, Tessa locked her front door and left for her first official day of work—well, orientation—a super-tight bundle of nerves. She headed for Lovebirds on foot, craving a coffee but knowing better. It'd set her heart sprinting and make her more agitated, whereas the exercise would hopefully dissipate some of her banked-up unexpended energy.

Given the pathways weren't too steep, she wouldn't get too sweaty and gross. She could arrive reasonably fresh, and psyched up, ready and extra raring to go.

The preliminary signs suggested a good, positive start—no rain, not too windy, and ultimately, she'd gotten the job. An all-around wonderful outcome, workwise. She'd lost track of how many times she'd pinched herself, still not quite believing the ensuing situation. But how would it affect her interactions with Gabe? Not that she expected him to have held a torch for her, as she had for him.

She continued along the sidewalk, taking a slow wide arc to the pier, and waved to Sabine, aka Bean, in barista mode behind the coffee machine, and her good friend Lavinia, who had just finished serving a customer at Nina's Bakery. The older owner, Zia Milla, was warm, friendly, and lovely, but her strong spiritual, almost pagan practices freaked out her niece, Lavinia, and Tessa too.

Tessa's mom had reveled in it. She'd been super involved with Zia Milla and a bunch of others, until she'd passed. Whereas Tessa believed it was better not to immerse herself in things she didn't understand, anything with no clear explanation. Her belief system warned her not to play with potentially fierce, uncontrollable fire and stick to science.

From the moment Tessa had met Lavinia, they'd had an instant affinity. Like her, Lavinia had also steered away from the occult. Nothing had compromised their friendship, thankfully. Once Tessa got through today, she'd give her friend a well overdue call and arrange a catch up, then update her on everything.

She strolled past Jemma's Blooms florist but couldn't see her owner friend, and continued along the street, the light breeze blowing her toward Lovebirds, the salty sea air stinging her nostrils. Contrary to her parents' beliefs back then, many a hot-blooded female found Gabe's personality irresistible.

As a whole, his drive, his persistence, his tough-love pursuit of excellence made him super appealing. Receiving a compliment from him meant everything because he didn't give them away. He'd only ever said what he meant. From what she'd witnessed he'd never used a false, strategic agenda to benefit him alone.

The sun shone on Lovebirds like a spotlight, directing her to the pier's new center stage. Seagulls flew by, attempting to steal fishermen's catches and hungry, careless tourists' unattended food, while the people in question took photos. So San Destino.

She hovered behind Lovebirds, not quite ready to go in, slinked up to the railing and stared out into the ocean. Would Gabe reconsider taking the plunge with her? She was already willing, and more than able, depending on how things played out.

Tessa needed to have a robust plan when it came to Gabe, something to reduce the risk of being undermined, of splitting them apart. Again. Some would say whatever happened constituted fate, but had her family played a physically interfering role? No amount of negative energy could have diverted Gabe's letter from a safe and timely delivery. So maybe the postal service was purely to blame, given the letter flew out of the crashed mail van.

The increasingly strong scent of salt-tinged spring air, mixed with freshly caught fish and the frequent cry of scavenger birds, reinforced her sense of home and awareness of things she'd taken for granted. Gabe returning had highlighted what required change, areas where she needed to start afresh.

No matter the time lapse since spending precious, intimate moments with him, no matter her regrets and wishes that their situation had transpired differently, they both had to take control and be responsible for all their decisions going forward, whether or not they reconnected on a romantic level.

The facts were, many a teenage romance failed. The data, the stats, supported that exact statement. And yet, what she'd felt for her high school sweetheart had lingered, been life-altering. It impacted her assessment of every other man she'd met since. She'd tried hard to replicate, and surpass, what she and Gabe had shared, but no other guy had come close.

Had she held onto her own sentimental reality? For sure. But now that he'd reappeared, along with his letter, they could speak in depth, and she could clarify the massive misunderstanding. They could possibly work toward reuniting … assuming that's what they both wanted and were free to do.

Romeo and Juliet-ish in its romantic impact, in this instance they'd thankfully survived to learn the truth. She crossed her fingers no other catastrophic weirdness occurred, even though she refused to partake in the San Destino spiritual shit. Ultimately, honest answers allowed them both the opportunity to make more informed choices.

Wave upon repetitive wave splashed against the wooden pier posts, sending a film of sea spray floating in the air ahead. She hoped to dodge the next bout of mist or else risk smelling like a seal. A memorable impression, but not quite the one she wanted to make on Gabe this time around.

With the weather warm and sunny and the winds died down, she'd chosen to wear a flowy long floral dress, practical and comfortable while keeping with the Lovebirds dress code and Gabe's likes, his long-ago preference for ultra-feminine attire. On her, anyway. And if nothing else, she wanted to establish an enticing platform to extract his truth.

The short walk, plus stopping to tune in to the natural rhythm of the sea, had reinvigorated her senses and calmed her anxiety. Connecting with the elements, with nature had provided just what she needed before embarking on all the sudden but exciting changes—new job, new prospects, Gabe's unexpected return.

Going by what she knew of him and his personality, his decision to reside in the mountains hadn't deviated too much from his teenage self. He'd require somewhere secluded, peaceful, quiet, a space allowing him downtime to re-energize. As outgoing and extroverted as he appeared, he shared her introverted heart.

She approached Lovebirds, stopped, and stared out across the bay. She gave herself a little last-second psych-up shake, then lifted her arms above her head for a grounding stretch.

"That sort of morning, is it?" She couldn't miss Gabe's telltale Scottish accent anywhere.

She whipped her head around to find the guy in question smirking, standing in the beer garden, chairs and tables half set up. The bar didn't start official service until Friday, but she presumed he needed to show the staff the full workings of the place and arrange a designated spot for them to congregate and eat.

On Monday, she'd seen the meeting room and glimpsed a staff kitchen area, but on such a lovely day, it'd be a shame to sit inside. He'd obviously thought the same.

"If you mean I'm preparing myself for today, then *yes*."

"Good answer."

"I figured you might approve."

"I do." He roved his gaze over her, subtly, appreciatively. "Come on in and have a coffee, while we wait for the rest of the newbies."

He disappeared inside and swung open the front door, gesturing for her to enter. His white chef jacket gleamed, contrasting with his black denim jeans, his uniform a unique departure from the stereotypical small checked black-and-white pants.

"Thank you." She smiled, her heart aflutter at his close proximity, her hyperawareness of his potent masculinity mixed with magical memories. "Are you cooking today?"

"I am. Thought I'd give you all a taste of the menu. Help you to know the dishes, what's on offer, what you'd recommend, depending on a patron's preferences and dietary requirements."

Such a great idea. She couldn't wait to sample his selections, see whether he'd retained some of that experimental raw passion. Not that he'd ever devised peculiar concoctions. He'd always preferred a fresh take on simple classics, trying a new complementary ingredient or playing around with presentation. She'd loved being his guinea pig and especially working off the calories afterward.

The roguish glint in his eye suggested he'd tapped into her train of thought, insinuating his thinking had also traveled down that trajectory. Not that it meant anything now, other than a mutual acknowledgment and appreciation of their shared past.

He pulled out a cool blue stool for her at the huge, circular bar, the standout centerpiece of the internal space. "Flat white?"

He'd remembered. "Yes, please. But decaf."

"Decaf?" His forehead creased with astonishment. She'd always loved caffeine.

"I don't want to be too wired." Or send her pulse pounding into heart attack territory.

"Fair enough. Two sugars?"

"Not anymore. Weaned myself off them a month ago."

"Good for you. I always thought you were sweet enough." His eyes crinkled with mischief, and he went into barista mode.

Oh. She shifted in her seat. Such a simple sentence, yet she'd read right into it. From the moment she'd arrived, they'd filled their conversation with a stream of innuendo. Or maybe that was her dirty mind's interpretation.

"Here you are." He'd made her coffee in a cup not a glass, as she'd always preferred, and included a mini melting moment on the saucer. Her favorite treat. Back when they were inseparable, they'd read an online Aussie recipe that Gabe had successfully tried and tweaked. "Enjoy."

"I will, thank you." She took a sip of her hot drink, had a bite of her biscuit, and sighed. So good. He'd always made her coffee, and everything else, exactly to her liking.

"I need to leave now, but I'll catch up with you again this afternoon, assuming that still suits."

"It does." They exchanged smiles. "I'll see you later." She looked forward to spending some private in-person time with him. She wanted to determine if that spark he'd reignited was real or a relic of the past.

While she finished her coffee and cookie, the rest of the staff straggled in, some making it right on the required dot. Some a smidge later.

Lewis wrangled the team into a space at the front of the bar and did a spiel on Lovebirds, including the mission and vision—and informed them where to find the code of conduct, and that it required their signature—as well as staff rights and the official complaints process.

Afterward, he took them on a thorough tour of the building, then went over the use of the computer-ordering software, and allocated table zones for service staff. Tomorrow, they'd have a faux run-through before the big Friday opening.

All de-caffeinated up and eager to get busy so the morning would pass quickly, Tessa volunteered for as many demonstrations and practice activities as possible.

Every single spot they assembled, a range of delicious scents wafted over. It got to almost 1:00 PM and her stomach growled. She'd pushed on as long as she could and now struggled to concentrate, struggled to ignore the incredible, enticing aromas.

Last, but definitely not least, Lewis emailed staff login info to the Lovebirds member section, giving them all access to agency specific information, including the orientation manual, then led them to the kitchen. She'd only half listened, eager to eat and get another glimpse of Gabe.

Lewis pushed open the doors and *wow!* The area buzzed with activity, chefs and cooks working in tandem like a well-oiled, well-programmed machine. Spacious and sparkling, with state-of-the-art appliances and a raw earthiness, the warm-but-crisp lighting had the space radiating enthusiasm, creativity, and innovation.

Like a true head chef, Gabe had everything under control, mastering the right balance of instruction, constructive feedback, encouragement, and motivation. She couldn't take her eyes off the enigmatic man, the man who'd never left her fantasies, her heart.

She may as well enjoy subtly ogling him while she could, because once they spoke, everything might change. And not necessarily for the better …whatever they each defined as 'better'.

Lewis spoke about the kitchen, its renovation, factoring in its historical standing, and the inclusion of modern appliances, but she'd hardly heard a word, thoroughly mesmerized by Gabe. Except he'd been too busy to send even a glance her way, which was both disappointing and impressive.

He demonstrated a passion for and dedication to his work. One hundred percent focus and concentration equaled super sexy in her mind. Because whatever lucky woman he chose, he'd show the same dedication, love, and appreciation.

At the end of his spiel, Lewis ushered the group through the expansive cooking zone and led them into the beer garden. They sat in the glorious sunshine and, minutes later, their all-day-breakfast sample plates started arriving.

Culinary staff carried a large platter to each table and laid it in the middle, like a mini buffet. Tessa scanned the options and gasped. The omelet. *Their* Lovebirds omelet sat right in the center as the focal point. He'd created that dish especially for her—two birds kissing—and presented it exactly as he had all those years ago.

Unbidden tears burned behind her eyes. Had he planned to serve it all along, or had he been inspired by seeing her again? Either way, raw emotion gripped her heart and squeezed. Staff at her table stared at her with perplexed expressions, so she grabbed a serving spoon and filled her plate with a range of items, diverting any further attention.

Bacon, chorizo, hash browns, spinach, tomatoes, baked beans, mushrooms and, of course, the omelet. Tessa tried hard to steady her shaking hand and hoped no one noticed. She tucked into the amazing offerings, leaving the Lovebirds omelet until last. She wanted to savor every single forkful.

She scooped the kissing-beak portion into her mouth, the slightly crispy outer texture and fluffy filling taking her straight back to the last time he'd served it to her. It had been delicious then and was extra delicious now. She closed her eyes and moaned.

Oh shit. Had anyone else heard? Her eyes sprang open to find Gabe standing beside her with a huge smirk.

"Sounds like you really enjoyed that."

A rush of heat filled her cheeks. He'd said those exact words to her twice in the past. The first time, after he'd fed her his Lovebirds omelet, and the second, after she'd given him her first ever blowjob. At the drive-in.

She'd lost interest in popcorn and craved him instead. Gabe had been the first guy to come in her mouth, and she'd loved it, licked him clean, thoroughly enjoying his flavor, sipping his pleasure. Did he still taste as good?

His gaze flicked to her lips and back to her eyes.

Her face heated further.

Lewis clapped his hands, startling her out of her Gabe spell. "For any of you who haven't yet met him, this is Gabe Raven, our head chef and owner. Any issues, come and speak to one of us."

Gabe rocked on his feet and grinned. "Hi, all, welcome aboard. Thanks for your interest in Lovebirds. Hope you enjoyed the food. I look forward to working with you."

"Hi, Gabe, the food is amazing!" one of the new staff called out.

Everyone else nodded and uttered sounds of appreciation.

"Thank you." Gabe gestured with his hands. He'd always struggled to speak without incorporating them into the mix to enhance his words. A European thing? Having grown up with Zia Milla as a close family friend, she'd seen the behavior strongly represented in the Italian culture.

"Right, folks, finish up. You've got ten more minutes, then we need to go through the stock ordering procedures." Lewis's no-nonsense voice broke through the chatter.

Gabe leaned down close to Tessa's ear. "When you're done, come and find me," he said, reiterating his instructions from the other night. His soft, sensual whisper, loud enough only for her to hear, had her subtly squeezing her thighs together.

She nodded and he retreated inside, out of sight.

****

Once everyone had left, Tessa located Gabe cleaning up in the kitchen. "I finally received your letter." Best to initially address the large, lingering elephant in the room, and see what transpired.

He snapped his head up, his face contorted with confusion. "My letter?"

"The one you sent years ago. The one asking me to meet you in Vegas. The one I never got until last week."

"You never… Your parents—?"

She shifted closer, careful to retain some distance until they'd cleared the long, California-haze clogged air. "No. At least, I don't think they had anything to do with it." She paused to gather her racing thoughts and order them into something coherent. "A mail truck accident on the bridge on Thursday had letters and flowers flying everywhere. Somehow, your note made it right to me. I know it sounds ridiculous."

"It does and it doesn't."

Her brow pulled together. "What do you mean?"

"I always thought this place had a freaky feel, whether I wanted to rationally accept it or not. It reminded me of Scotland, but a more modern version. Less architectural history, less deep-rooted superstition, but a similar vibe." He stopped scrubbing the stove and discarded the scourer on the stainless-steel bench top. "And I met you."

What did that mean? "Sorry?"

He stepped forward and stared into her eyes, his hands expressive as always. "I'd moved around so much it was hard to make friends, let alone consider the possibility of a girlfriend."

"Oh." She glanced at the spotless, gleaming floor. "When I didn't get your letter, I thought you'd found someone else."

"And I thought you had. I was devastated. Hurt. Frustrated."

Her eyes darted up to meet his. "Angry?"

"At you. No. Never. At my parents for forcing me away, yes."

She averted her stare to her fidgety fingers. "I tried to call you, you know. After I got over the heartbreak."

"But the number was disconnected, yes?"

She swung her gaze up to meet his and nodded.

"I'd gone into the army and my parents moved again almost straight away."

She let out a sigh, a bittersweet smile seizing her lips. "A comedy of errors."

"Far from a comedy." He dragged his hand through his hair. "Fuck." He walked right up to her and looked her in the eye. "I can't tell you how brilliant it is, how much of a relief, to hear you didn't decide against me." He bounced on the spot. "I've missed you so fucking much."

"Me too."

He stepped back, as though forcefully pushing himself from her personal space. "Are you with someone?"

"No. You?"

"No." He shook his head, his hands doing a whole 'no way' motion. "Ever been married?"

"Never."

"Me either. Children?"

"No. You?"

"Not that I'm aware of." He charged forward and grabbed her face with both hands. "Can I kiss you?"

She nodded, unable to speak, and he planted a claiming kiss on her mouth.

Tessa moaned at his urgent onslaught and melted into him, their tongues frantic, searching, desperate. It went beyond what they'd previously shared. He pressed her back against the wall, their torsos glued together, his erection nudging her, hard and insistent.

The kiss turned combustible, his hands all over her, tearing at her clothes, their bodies undulating, seeking friction. Entirely alone, they were seconds away from fucking in his sparkling stainless-steel kitchen. And she couldn't wait.

He trailed his lips along her jaw, to her ear, down her neck, his nips beyond nibbling, bordering on greedy gulps. And she loved it. Loved his touch. It had always sparked every single cell in her body to life.

He stripped her dress over her head and flung it across the room, leaving her in her skimpy white lace bra and briefs.

Gabe growled. "Fuck me. Fucking gorgeous." He unfastened her bra and threw it off. Before she could gasp, he sucked a nipple into his mouth, his incredible fingers tweaking and teasing the other until she thought she might come purely from breast play.

A first. Everything a first and last with him.

He kissed his way down her stomach until he kneeled before her, his fingers hooked into her panties. "May I?"

"Yes!" She didn't even have to think. He'd obliterated all her inhibitions. Both as a teenager and now. Only Gabe had shown that power.

Slowly, gently, he eased off the scrap of lace, leaving her totally bare. For his eyes only. She hoped no one with keys came back to check on anything. Though, at this point, he'd worked her up so much, she almost didn't care if anyone saw.

"Mmm … beautiful." He nuzzled her mound with his nose, then his slightly stubbled cheek, kissing the smooth skin thoroughly, reverently, skipping her clit and tantalizing her inner thighs with erotic bites, sucks, and licks.

The kitchen echoed with her sounds of pleasure.

"Lift your leg over my shoulder. I need to taste you."

Gabe didn't have to ask again. He'd already taken her to a shameless level, so shameless, she bucked into his face, begging for more.

And like he always had, he delivered.

He licked her entrance, the tip of his tongue penetrating, thrusting, shallow, deep, devouring her like a starving, ravenous man presented with a banquet. The moment her moans got loud, he glided his moist lips over her folds and swiped a leisurely lick over her throbbing clit.

She came instantly and he sucked her into his mouth, driving her deeper into ecstasy. If it wasn't for his strong hands holding her hips, and her fingers threaded into his hair, she'd have crumpled to the floor.

So good. Better than good. Incredible. Their exploratory adolescent phase had been amazing, but this … wow. She slumped against the wall, thoroughly spent, thoroughly satisfied. Still panting.

Gabe eased her leg down and stood, still fully clothed, still in control. He kissed her, but it suddenly felt distant.

He pulled back, his jaw tight, their bodies no longer touching. "I'm sorry. I got carried away. I shouldn't have done that. I'm your boss. It's not right."

Yes, it was. What they'd just shared exemplified right. So very, very right. "Not right? Is that how you assessed my response?"

He shoved a hand through his messy blond hair and took another step back. "I'm not saying we don't have chemistry, but you're working for me. And we need to get to know each other again. We can't rely on our raging pubescent hormones and wishful memories from the past to guide our future."

Oh. Vulnerability seeped through her, dampening her high. She slipped away from the cold wall and snatched up her clothes, unable to speak further until she'd dressed.

He silently watched her the whole time, unable to

stand still. He'd always expended a lot of energy, struggled to stay in one spot, but this time, discomfort, and was that a hint of regret, vibrated from his body.

She slung her bag over her shoulder and strode out of the kitchen. She loved Gabe, well, teenage Gabe, but she'd matured past the point of game playing. Either he wanted to give them a chance or he didn't. The sooner they both knew the answer, the better.

"Where are you going?" His footsteps thudded behind her. "Wait."

She stopped, drew in a centering breath, and swung around to face him. His blond hair stuck up at all odd angles, disheveled from her passion-filled grip plus him raking his hand through it, repeatedly. "What do you want?"

He thrust his fidgety hands in his pockets, his gaze locking on hers. "You. But for the right reasons. My decision-making can't be based off nostalgia and dreams."

"So, what are you saying?"

"In order to know whether things can work now, we can't make choices off hope. Off wanting to recreate the past. Chemistry and connection are essential but equally as important as rational and cogent considerations."

She tugged on the strap of her handbag. What he said made logical sense, but what did it look like in reality? "So, what does that entail?"

"We date. On the down-low. No need for anyone else to know at this stage. Let us work out whether we're still aligned. It's been a long time since we knew each other, and we've both had different experiences that have helped us grow. But it doesn't mean we've grown in the same direction."

As much as it hurt her ego, he was right. They

couldn't establish a strong foundation from a flimsy, untested base. They needed to reacquaint themselves, determine if what they shared these days had any substance. "Fine. I'll let you lead. See you in the morning." For the Lovebirds opening dress rehearsal. She spun back to the exit.

"Come to my place for dinner tomorrow night. After work."

What? "I'll see..." She stopped, her hand on the doorknob. "Text me your address."

"Is that a *yes*?"

She sighed but didn't turn around. "Yes," she said, and left before she ran back into his big, strong arms.

Chapter Seven

Gabe exhaled with a fuck-ton of grateful relief. The staff had aced the Thursday practice run. Taking it in turns to act as customers, allowed each employee to go through the requirements of their role and become familiar with the equipment and practical processes, ready for the Lovebirds official opening. Hopefully, the venue would be rammed full of people—a mix of locals and tourists—creating his exact envisioned vibe.

And Tessa had agreed to come over to his place for dinner. A personal and professional win. Two goals he'd set out to achieve, and hoped to realize, not just mentally, emotionally but also physically. Since he'd seen her, she'd infiltrated his system like an uncontrollable addiction.

Other than doing the required schmoozing with contractors and staff, he'd been stuck sweating in the kitchen and had hardly seen his love. But he'd see her tonight at his home, just the two of them, alone. They still had a lot to talk about to confirm their compatibility. Yet his body craved her touch.

Their mini confrontation, after he'd eaten her out, had left him with an unrelenting hard-on. He wanted her so fucking bad. His dick throbbed with need, driven to pound into her. But as a fucking mature man, he couldn't give in to lust. He had to show some control.

Or he'd need to get into the habit of jerking himself off before her presence screwed with his ability to think clearly. He had to ensure he got into the right frame of mind to make the best decisions for them both.

The second she'd left Lovebirds last evening, he'd somehow made it home, still in a lustful daze. He'd gone inside, leaned his back against the door, ripped opened his fly, freed his confined cock, and gone to town.

The epic release had hit the required spot … for a few minutes. The pleasurable relief only lasted until he remembered her writhing and whimpering with his face buried between her legs.

"Jesus fucking Christ." He thrust the tray of meatloaf and veggies—her favorite of his main dishes back in the day—into his oven, the heat pouring over his face, arms, and torso. He shut the door and tried to tame his over-eager dick. He had to focus on tonight. She'd arrive at any moment, so he needed to get his head together. His bollocks in check.

He set the timer for forty-five minutes, grabbed a beer from the fridge, propped his ass against the counter, and waited. The refreshing brew cooled his Tessa fever. For now. Hopefully it'd help prevent him from accosting her with an urgent kiss the second she stepped through his front door. Fingers fucking crossed.

With only a quarter of his pale ale left, tires crunched along the driveway. He gulped the rest of his drink and dropped the empty bottle into the recycling bin right as the doorbell rang. Gabe blew out a big get-your-act-together breath.

Once he let her in, he'd go to the fridge and grab the small charcuterie board he'd prepared for an appetizer, even though he'd rather have another taste of her sweet pussy.

Nerves swooped in his stomach. He answered the door and … fuck. His smile morphed into an 'O' of awe. Gabe scanned over her, totally lost, unable to pull together a sensible string of words, his usually sharp brain shutting down. She stood before him in a simple, halter-neck black-and-floral summer dress with plenty of cleavage. She'd gone and pulled out the mega big guns, making him muff-struck mute.

"Hi." Her husky voice spoke straight to his cock.

He shook the lustful fog from his mind and gestured for her to enter, her strappy sandals clacking against the floorboards. "You look gorgeous." With her walking ahead of him, he couldn't help but admire her amazing ass.

"Thank you. I, um … I brought a salad. Shall I put it in the fridge? I haven't dressed it yet." He'd have been equally happy, ecstatic, if she hadn't dressed either.

She emptied the contents out of a large black bag that he hadn't even noticed. He'd been too mesmerized by her absolute beauty.

How the fuck could he keep his hands off her? He'd already failed once. And if that meant failure, he wanted to fail every fucking day. But he'd sworn to suss things out, not get too caught up too quickly. Except, with her looking so captivating and smelling so fucking sexy, he had close to no chance of keeping her out of his bed. "Leave it on the bench, my darling."

She swung around and fixed a lifted-eyebrow stare on him. "Darling?"

"Old habits and all that…" Because yeah, he'd used the endearing term when they'd been together back in their teens. And he still meant it, no matter how sensible and rational he attempted to act.

He closed his eyes briefly and tried to clear his Tessa-overloaded brain. "Dinner won't be long."

Her captivating gaze reconnected with his, sending a jolt of undeniable attraction zinging through his whole body. From the moment he'd met her, she'd fucking made positive, permanent, everlasting changes, right down to his DNA.

Their reunion reinforced he couldn't continue with his outdated, delusional mentality—believing he could move forward without her. In some way, he needed

Tessa in his life. The universe had proven its point.

However, before he dove into the romantic waters with both eager feet a second time, he had to ensure his decision-making wasn't fueled by lust, sentimentality, and reminiscence.

Because, yeah, their attraction could have lit up the whole of San Destino. Still could. It could have lit up the whole of North America. But was that powerful force enough to hold them together long term?

She stood behind the counter, salad bowl in front of her, dressing condiments to the right, her waiting gaze trained on him as if to say, *what-the-fuck-now*?

His thoughts exactly. If he went with his gut, he'd wrap her in his arms and kiss the ever-loving fuck out of her. He wanted to have Tessa as his decadent appetizer, second night in a row. Fuck me, he couldn't get the taste of her out of his head, her whimpers, her cries of pleasure while his mouth took her to paradise.

His dick barred up, eager to do it all over again. Then after she climaxed, he'd draw her down onto his cock so she could ride out another orgasm, but this time with him joining in. He went to step past her and swallowed, trying to stop ogling her sexy body. "Let me check—"

She slammed her mouth onto his, blocking his path to the stove, her tongue driving the atmosphere up to sizzling, blazing, burning any route back to normality. He should stop her, attempt to tap into some sensibility, shift her aside and check on their food. But he couldn't. He couldn't get enough of her.

Gabe grasped her head with one hand and her ass with the other and delved his tongue deeper into her sweet, sexy mouth. Her hot little moan got his dick ramrod hard, and he ripped off her underwear and raised her onto the counter.

She lifted her dress, leaned back on one hand, and spread her legs. Tessa on a platter. His own private, fantasy menu. His own delicious feast. He should be cautious, patient, stave off giving into his desires, but he couldn't. With her right there in front of him, offering herself with utter trust and abandon, he couldn't say *no*. As always, sweet Tessa teased and tempted him beyond reason.

He bent down between her legs and latched his mouth onto her clit, flicking his tongue firm, hard, and fast. In under a minute, she came. Twice. Male fucking pride to the max.

Gabe grabbed her off the counter, into his arms, and strode straight to his bedroom to give her a thorough, pleasurable pounding.

"Wait!"

He stopped, abiding by her wishes, and hoped now that he'd given over to his feelings, she hadn't changed her mind about going further. But if she had, he'd honor her decision.

"Don't you have to check on dinner?"

Dinner. Oh yeah. He turned with her still in his arms, switched off the oven and timer, and continued directly to his bedroom. They both needed this. They both needed to determine if a relationship between them now was feasible physically, mentally, emotionally, and spiritually.

Gabe sat her on the edge of his bed. "Take your dress off."

She did and *oh fuck*. Gorgeous. Stunning. Breathtaking. Yes, he'd seen her naked yesterday, but having her fully bare on his brand-spanking-new mattress had his fantasy meeting reality in a better-than-ever-anticipated way.

He shrugged off his clothes and went to join her,

but she held out her hand to stop him. "I need to suck your cock first."

Fuck me. Yes, fucking please. He stood right in front of her and she gripped his erection, sliding her palm all the way up and over his length. So fucking good. She slowly pumped and squeezed and teased, driving him right to the brink. Then she added her mouth.

The warmth, the wetness, the passion.

He held her head and thrust between her lips, just how she'd liked it. Him too. Nostalgia met present need and he came on her tongue, in her mouth. She moaned and swallowed every single drop.

Fucking brilliant. Mind-blowing. "On your back, my darling." Because he needed more of her, his body frantic to fill her right up.

She repositioned herself so she lay in the center of the bed, keeping her legs bent and spread wide for his pleasure. And didn't he fucking appreciate her openness, her trust. She'd offered him the best, most delicious view he could ever want, reinvigorating his dick.

Gabe rolled on a condom and climbed between her thighs, aligned his cock with her moist entrance and thrust home. She mewled and bucked into him, with more freedom, abandon, and confidence than he remembered.

He could be jealous that she'd had other lovers, but it would serve no purpose. Greater events had played out to bring them here, to bring them back to each other. Whether for a short time or a long time, he didn't know. But he could focus on the moment and make the most of whatever encounters they were destined to have together.

Their joining transcended time, place … everything. As it always had with her, and even more so now, it epitomized perfection. The brilliance of their bond was impossible to deny. She would forever remain a huge, immeasurable impact on his life.

They crested on a wave of absolute bliss, and finally came together. Their recovering breaths intermingled and he kissed her, adoringly, reverently, with the utmost respect, and, *fuck me*, love.

"Stay right where you are, my darling. I'll sort this out and be right back." He took off to his en suite, disposed of the condom, and deliberated about how best to proceed. Should he rejoin her and have a second helping—ridiculously tempting—or serve her dinner in bed, re-energize them enough to talk about how they both envisaged their futures?

He took a good, hard, discerning look at himself in the mirror. Yes, he'd aged—cavernous wrinkles crinkling his forehead, grooves cutting into the corners of his eyes and lips—they both had, but they still shared a special magic.

However, now, instead of fumbling through and learning what it took to please, they both had the skills and experience to take their intimate interaction to a whole other, earth-shattering level.

Gabe re-entered his bedroom. Instead of diving into his insatiable desire for Tessa, he'd let her choose how she'd prefer to proceed. "Would you like to have something to eat?"

Her eyes dipped to his dick and she licked her lips. "I sure would."

His laugh came out raspy, needy, longing to let her please him again. But that wouldn't help either of them determine whether this thing between them was a short-term nostalgic fling or something sustainable.

He tried to tame his cock. "Are you hungry?"

"I believe I already answered that question."

"Tessa." He put on his best *be serious* facial expression.

She crawled to the edge of the bed, stayed on all

fours, and stared into his eyes with unmistakable want. Could she sense the desperation for more sensual exploration, more sex, in him too?

"Maybe we *should* have some food. Give us more energy to expend later." The soft, throaty tone of her voice made him want to say *bugger the food and gorge on me*. Again.

Instead of giving in to his inner devil, he extended his hand. "Come with me." And he meant that literally and figuratively.

She immediately interlocked her fingers with his, and he led her into the kitchen. Gabe directed her to a seat at his dining table, made the salad, then retrieved the meatloaf and veggies from the oven and plated their meals.

He'd decided against feeding her in bed because, going by their reaction to one another, they'd dump their dinner on the bedside tables and prioritize tucking into each other. This way, it reduced the risk of succumbing to overwhelming want. But it didn't make it impossible. Maybe he should have insisted they threw on some clothes first.

Ridiculous. They were grown adults. Surely, they could hold off on devouring each other for ten minutes while they ate. Gabe couldn't decide who needed more convincing—him or her.

He really should have put on an apron rather than risk burning his family jewels, but too late now—their plates sat on the counter with wisps of steam winding up toward the ceiling. Using the juices from the meatloaf tray, he made a gravy and poured it into a small ceramic jug—she'd always preferred sauces on the side.

Gabe placed their plates, the salad bowl, and the gravy boat on the table.

"You remembered." A huge, surprised smile filled

her face.

"I did." His memories of Tessa were etched deep into his soul. Was it the same for her?

He sat next to his dream woman and poured a generous serving of gravy onto his meatloaf and veggies, while she'd sparingly covered just her meat. Tessa had always disliked her food touching, but occasionally dared to dip a bit of baked potato into the gravy. People's eating habits fascinated him, particularly hers. In all truth, everything about her fascinated him.

They ate their meals in relative silence, well, except for her moans of appreciation. With her eyes closed, and the eager way she sucked every last morsel of food off her fork, he could hardly sit still. He couldn't wait to taste more of her.

She swallowed, sliced a piece of crispy, caramelized potato, and popped it into her mouth. "Mmm, so delicious."

He almost expected her to come right there at the table. And wouldn't that be extra hot.

His cooking had always hit exactly the right spot for her, and her enthusiasm had encouraged him to pursue his culinary degree and become a head chef. She'd rarely rated anything he produced below a nine out of ten, which thoroughly fed his ego.

He returned to eating the rest of his dinner, enjoying her little oralgasmic show, and especially her bare body. Unfortunately, the table blocked his view of her from the waist down. But he'd rectify that as soon as they were done. Dessert could wait until way later, and he'd sort out the dishes tomorrow.

Fuck. He'd been so caught up he hadn't even offered her a drink. "Wine, water—"

"Just you." She met his gaze, her usually hazel eyes looked like molten pools of licorice. And although he adored their natural golden-honey warmth, he fucking loved licorice.

Gabe stood so fast, his chair toppled over, crashing onto the timber floor. He lunged forward, lifted her up, folded her over his shoulder, and returned to his bedroom to indulge in his own, mouthwatering, non-food sweet.

Chapter Eight

Tessa woke up in Gabe's bed, his body wrapped around hers like a cinnamon twist. So much had changed and yet stayed the same—his passion, his sexy Scottish accent, his intense, focused attention on her and her needs.

He'd been hesitant, reluctant for them to get re-involved too quickly, but their chemistry made it inevitable. For her, it superseded lust, superseded rekindling their past. They'd both matured, experienced life, and yet circumstances had brought them back together.

Was it a test to confirm whether their connection had a special, unbreakable bond? Because she loved him. Then and now. Although she'd never believed in the whole *spiritual side* of San Destino, refused to accept any of the *mystical* stuff, being reunited with Gabe had her wondering whether it held some truth. It made her question whether maybe some greater forces were at play, beyond the reach and full understanding of human society.

Gabe stirred and held her tighter, his morning wood digging into her butt. "You awake?"

She definitely was now, his hot breath scorching the rim of her ear, making her super horny. Again. "Yes."

Gabe sigh-groaned. "I'm so glad you stayed, my darling." He kissed along her neck, his hands clasping and kneading her breasts.

And—Oh. My. God.—it felt so amazingly good. Beyond any words. "Me too. We never got around to dessert."

"Oh yes, we did. In fact, I can do with another helping." He kissed down her spine, spread her legs, and licked into her core.

She gasped, and he glided his tongue over and around her clit, licking and sucking until she climaxed.

Gabe growled. "That's it. That's it. I need your taste on my tongue."

He took her right to full-blown ecstasy, then broke away briefly to roll on a condom. Thrusting his cock inside her, he stayed along for the amazing ride, until they both re-emerged from the depths of an unforgettable interconnection.

She lay there, panting, while he ran his hands along her body and uttered sweet, sexy, soothing words. His attentive, passionate presence made her feel amazing, but she needed to know he wouldn't revert to his too-cautious self. She needed to know whether to let her heart go all in or remain wary.

"I could do this all day, but we need to get ready for the opening."

Oh, her opening was more than ready for him. Again. But he didn't mean *her*, unfortunately.

Gabe went to roll away and stopped. "Oh, and remember, this … eventuation is between us for now. Yes?"

Way to ruin the moment. "I understand." Though she burst at her barely stitched-together seams to tell her close female friends—Bean, Jemma, Tildie, and especially Lavinia. Since Lavinia had moved to town, they'd struck up a strong friendship, sharing an aversion to all the San Destino spiritual hoo-ha. What would she think of Tessa's reconnection with Gabe?

Tessa could be patient, for a little while. If Gabe truly loved her, he wouldn't want to keep their relationship a secret for long. Right?

Upon his insistence, they arrived at work separately and went about their roles. He hovered in the kitchen, while she managed the front of house, greeting, seating, and serving eager, excited customers. Long-standing residents of San Destino, as well as newcomers, had flocked to see the refurbished, highly anticipated Lovebirds.

An elegant, attractive woman in her mid-thirties, possibly early forties, entered the establishment, her dark curly hair swept into a ponytail, and requested a table in the super-packed venue. She hadn't made a reservation, but something in Tessa insisted she allocate her a space. Not that she believed in intuition and all that crap.

She showed the well-dressed woman to a window seat that had just opened up, overlooking the sea, and the customer gently touched Tessa's hand, an indescribably intense jolt of awareness anchoring her to the spot. A few seconds ticked by before she could snap out of the overwhelming state and conjure up any words, any sentences that made sense. "What would you like?"

The woman's stare pierced through Tessa's tentative eye contact, her expression *knowing*, as though she could read her thoughts. "What would *you* like?"

Gabe.

It was the first and only word that came to mind. The only thing, the only person, she'd ever wanted with her whole heart. Even though they'd only recently reconnected after such a long time apart, as crazy as it sounded, this man was her everything.

The woman smiled. "You have a pure, open spirit. Gabe is a great match for you."

Had she said his name out loud to the lady? She was sure she hadn't. "How did you…?"

Gabe appeared from the kitchen and headed toward the intriguing consumer with a big, broad grin. "So good to finally meet you in person, Veronica. Thanks so much for coming." He shook her hand and she pulled him in for an affectionate, platonic hug.

Veronica, as in the renowned San Destino psychologist-turned-real-estate mogul? He must have used her to find his home. How else could he know the woman?

"I'm so glad I could make the opening."

"Me too. Thank you for clueing me in to the cabin availability and getting it sorted in my absence. It's everything I'd wished for, everything I'd dreamed about."

"I'm so happy it's working out well for you. How about Tessa?"

He stared at the woman with a confused, semi-stressed look on his spellbinding face. "What do you mean?"

"Have you given her what she wants? What she needs? What you both need?"

Gabe fixed an accusatory gaze on Tessa. "What did you tell her?"

"Nothing, I swear." Tessa refocused on Veronica and forced a smile. "He's given me exactly what I want, so far."

Veronica peered at Gabe. "If you plan to keep good staff, a great partner, you need to show you value them. You need to push past fear and admit your true feelings."

He swallowed and glanced around the busy room. "Ah … what can I get you?"

Deflection to the max. The woman had somehow known how to press right on his weakest point and confront him without being combative. A fantastic skill Tessa wished she possessed. Maybe she should grab Veronica's details and ask if she could sign up for some mentoring.

"The Lovebirds omelet please."

The meal Tessa and Gabe shared a special spot for, the first one they truly connected over. The dish she and Gabe loved.

How had this customer tuned in so closely to them? Had she somehow absorbed their thoughts and energy by psychic osmosis? No. Tessa refused to believe that. The idea alone pushed her thinking into the too 'out there' basket. More likely, the woman excelled at observation, at sensing the bond between people. Unsurprising, considering her psychology background.

"Great choice," Gabe said and took off back to his safe space—the same avoidance technique he'd used as a teenager to shut down any opportunity to further grill him and his thinking. Cooking had always provided him an escape. The one place he'd explained gave him safety, security, comfort.

Tessa collected some composure. "Would you like a drink?"

Veronica looked her in the eye. "I'll have a Cupid's Kiss please."

What? Tessa tried not to let her mouth gape open. That was the name of one of the new cocktails she had planned to introduce to their drinks menu. Was this just a string of coincidences or could this woman actually read people's minds? Although Tessa didn't believe in that rubbish, this lady was starting to freak her out.

Tessa turned to walk to the bar, and Veronica touched her arm. "Don't give up on what you desire."

She met the intriguing woman's steady, unwavering stare. "I don't intend to." Not unless Gabe told her with absolute certainty that he didn't want them to pursue a relationship. Tessa had everything crossed his fear wouldn't drive him down that dead-end road.

"Good. Passion, persistence, and perseverance breed success."

"I agree." Tessa's whole arm tingled, sending a flood of euphoria through her body.

Clarity infiltrated her thoughts, and she suddenly had no doubt that she and Gabe were destined to be together. Now she just had to allay his fears, his concerns, and convince him that he could take a chance on her, on them, this time.

"Tessa?" Gabe's gruff, sexy voice drew her gaze from the cocktail she'd half made. "Can I talk to you for two seconds?"

"Let me finish this, then I'll be right with you. Meet in your office?"

"Yeah."

What did he need to speak to her about so urgently?

She finished the cocktail, delivered it to Veronica, and made her way to join Gabe. He'd left his office door ajar and paced across the room.

"Come in." He stopped and stared directly into her eyes. "And shut the door."

She did as he asked and he stalked over to her, planting a hot-as-fuck kiss on her lips, his body pressing her hard against the closed door.

"Come to my place tonight." He slammed his mouth back onto hers before she could reply.

Tessa moaned and wrapped her arms around his neck. "I want to—"

"I hear a *but*." His eyes searched hers.

"I'll meet you there later. I'm catching up with some close friends for drinks and possibly dinner first."

"Where?"

"Here."

He kissed her again, slow, enticing, and erotic. Possessive, in a positive way. "Well, enjoy, my darling. And I'll look forward to having some more fun with you afterward." He patted her ass. "Now get back to work."

She laughed, gave him a quick, *ciao*-for-now kiss, and returned to the bar, hoping Veronica's prediction was accurate.

The rest of Tessa's shift went by without any more strange incidents, and no other Gabe sightings, unfortunately. Right as she was due to finish, her friends arrived, except Tildie who'd let her know she'd drop by later. She shouldn't say anything about her and Gabe rekindling their relationship, had thought she'd convinced herself not to, but she needed some advice. And she could trust her besties to keep her secret.

Tessa joined Jemma, Bean, and Lavinia in front of their allocated booth and gave each of them a hug. Instead of their regular jeans and t-shirts, they'd all dressed in stylish summer dresses.

They slid onto the cool blue leather seats, the tealight candles flickering on the table between them, and all started talking at once. The usual. They had always been a cheerful, caring, welcoming bunch. It was a privilege and an absolute pleasure to be part of the loyal, supportive little group.

"So, Tessa, how's the new job?" Jemma's penetrating eyes bore right into her brain, as though searching for a full account of the situation, as though sensing there was more to it than just work. Had Tessa's body language given away more than she'd realized?

"Was that your chef disappearing into the kitchen? He's hot!" Lavinia's big brown eyes sparkled with mischief.

Tessa laughed, her cheeks burning, throbbing, meaning they'd glow a telltale red.

"You're doing him!" Jemma propped her elbows on the table and leaned in, her long wavy brown hair falling forward.

"You are, aren't you?" Bean stared at her with wide, don't-even-try-to-deny-it eyes.

Tessa held up her hands in a stop-right-there gesture, unable to contain the excitement bubbling in her stomach. "Let me say something!"

They all fixed their gazes on her, silent and eager for her response.

"But I'll organize some drinks first." Because she needed time to know how to best broach the Gabe subject.

"Tessa!" a couple of them said in unison, shaking their heads.

With a cheeky smile, she took off for the bar. She needed a minute or two to sift through her jumble of thoughts and calm her heart. She needed to pull together some sort of grown-woman control. She needed to come up with some unbiased questions to obtain helpful, positive, actionable results.

After pouring a full serve of her friends' drinks of choice—Moscato for Jemma, Aperol Spritz for Lavinia, Cosmopolitan for Bean, and a Burning History cocktail for her, she carried them back on a tray. At the table, she handed out each glass and squished back in beside Bean.

Tessa expected an interrogation, but instead they caught up on everyone else's news—their love lives, the recent baseball scores, not that all of them were as interested as her—and discussed the weird accident on the bridge that had instigated this whole Tessa-Gabe reunion.

"Did you hear that Frankie has returned to town? I saw her and Nate at the supermarket checkout the other day and the scorching-hot spark between them could have melted the self-serve." Bean fanned her face.

"Maybe they'll get a second chance at a happily ever after? It feels like the season for rekindling romance." Jemma's all-seeing blue eyes drew her in, shining with an otherworld sort of wisdom.

Jemma and Bean glanced at each other with a conspiratorial grin, then focused on Tessa. "Speaking of romance, you never confirmed or denied your *situation* with the chef." Bean pinned her with her don't-even-try-to-bullshit-me gaze.

"Gabe is..." She sighed. Time to come clean. "Remember the guy I told you about when I was in secondary school?"

"The one you dated, *l'uomo scomparso*—the man who disappeared?" Lavinia's forehead furrowed.

"His family moved and we lost touch, yes. He said he'd contact me about meeting up, but I never received anything. Then the day the accident on the bridge happened, bursting open the back of that undelivered-mail truck, his misplaced letter somehow blew into my arms."

"So he had sent something. That's so romantic!" Lavinia leaned her elbows on the table and propped her face in her hands, sighing and staring up to the sky, looking totally dreamy.

The back of Tessa's eyes burned with lingering grief. "It is, and it isn't. It's equally amazing and disappointing. So many wasted years..."

"But it was out of your—*come si dice*, ah, how do you say?—control." Lavinia's concerned expression had Tessa's tears mounting, ready to roll onto her cheeks.

"It wasn't the right timing." Jemma's gentle, confident tone made her statement sound like fact.

Bean's brown eyes filled with tenderness. "Maybe you both needed to experience life and be in the right frame of mind."

An errant tear trickled down Tessa's face, clinging onto her jaw, and she brushed it away. All of the above and more. But things weren't as simple as them restarting where they'd left off.

Tessa swilled the rest of her Burning History cocktail in an attempt to strengthen her resolve. "Just between us, Gabe and I … we have been together. Recently." And yet it felt like forever since they'd last touched. "And he's invited me over to his house after this, but—"

Lavinia touched her hand. "But what?"

"He isn't as certain as me. I'm ready to jump right back in and announce to everyone that we're a couple, but he's hesitant. I'm not even supposed to tell anyone we're involved. I had to, though. I need your help, your ideas, your guidance regarding how to show him we're meant for each other." She needed to convince him that things would work out now. Second time lucky.

"Oh. So he's enjoying the sex but can't commit?" Bean's brow crinkled with worry, her auburn hair looking extra fiery under the LED lights.

"Honestly, we're both enjoying the sex." Tessa's cheeks flared with heat. "I'm one hundred percent committed to him, and I think he wants to be with me, but after what happened in the past, I'd say he's scared." Almost superstitious.

"Why don't you speak to Zia Milla? Get her opinion." Jemma's smile matched her gentle, encouraging tone.

"You know I'm not into *that* stuff."

Jemma fixed a calm, soothing, almost-hypnotic stare on Tessa. "Just because science can't make sense of something doesn't mean it doesn't exist."

Bean raised an eyebrow, a cheeky grin on her face. "Or that you can't hedge your practical-versus-spiritual bets."

Tessa had always focused on logical thinking, but

her friends had a point. Scientists constantly made new discoveries. They didn't know everything. Never claimed to.

Ultimately, whether she believed in something or not, she could consider it as just another opinion. It didn't mean she had to take the information as gospel. Having an open attitude couldn't cause any harm, right?

Except her mom had been caught up with Zia Milla and look what had happened to her and Tessa's dad. Not that Tessa believed all that evil-eye craziness, nor had faith in anything that had no factual founding.

Lavinia's eyes widened and she stared at the entrance. "Oh *Dio!*"

Tessa darted her gaze to the door and Lavinia's aunty walked in as if on cue. Speaking of the matriarch of superstition… The timing was impeccable, as if the woman had somehow tuned into their discussion.

Jemma's fingers clamped onto Tessa's wrist like pincers. "This is your chance. You may as well speak to her."

Bean and Lavinia sat there stunned into silence.

Tessa glanced at each of her friends, in turn, their faces filled with reassurance and love. She psyched herself up and walked over to the woman, intercepting her before she reached the bar. "Hi, Zia Milla."

SANDRA CARMEL

Chapter Nine

A sincere smile lit up the elegant, gray-haired woman's face, and she wrapped Tessa in a warm, affectionate hug. "Tessa, *bella*. It'sa been too long."

Tessa had always loved her Italian accent. In all her years in America, the lady had never lost it. Her distinctive voice, coupled with her European culture made her interesting, special, a standout. It added to her allure. And created part of the reason Tessa had stayed away. Zia Milla's charm was beyond engaging, more like captivating, mesmerizing.

"It has. How did the charity event go? I would have loved to have been there, but with Lovebirds—"

"I understand." Her smile transformed into a knowing grin. She took a seat at the bar. "It went well, *bella*. I look forward to you-a being involved next-a time."

"Yes. Let me know when you've organized another fundraiser."

"I will."

She needed to divert the conversation before Zia Milla said something unnervingly spooky. "What would you like to drink?"

"Let me see." Zia Milla reviewed the cocktail menu and pointed to the Grande Dame. "This one, *per favore*."

How very appropriate. Tessa shifted behind the bar, made the woman's requested drink, and handed it to her.

"*Grazie, bella*." Zia Milla smiled and stirred the cocktail with her straw.

They engaged in general chit chat, and Tessa let her know Lavinia and the rest of their girlfriend group were at a booth across from the bar.

Zia Milla turned and waved, then started on her cocktail. "This *è* incredible, *bella*. Thank you."

Gabe appeared, catching Tessa's eye in the background and she beckoned him over. She refocused on Zia Milla and couldn't contain her excited, I-can't-hide-my-love-for-this-guy grin. Seeing him always gave her exhilarating goosebumps. "Remember Gabe? He's the new owner and head chef."

"Oh, *si*. You—how do you say?—look *e* the same *ma* older." She sipped the remainder of her drink through the red-heart paper straw, jumped up from her bar stool, and engulfed him in an embrace.

In seconds, she pulled back with a start. "You are destined to be here." She studied his eyes. "You know what I mean. You connect. The energy *e* … aligned. In harmony." Zia Milla touched his forearm. "The mystical winds, they, how do you say? Were driven by you, by your passion, your desire."

He stared at her with confusion marring his already super-creased forehead. He'd ditched his white chef coat and looked just as delectable dressed in jeans and a t-shirt.

"You will understand." She gestured to Tessa. "She may not."

Zia Milla leaned in and whispered in Gabe's ear. She stepped away and sent him a secretive smile, said goodbye to Tessa and her girlfriends, then left.

Tessa fixed an interrogative stare on her love. "What did she say?"

"I'll tell you later. I need to handover to my sous chef and get going." A smile twitched on his lips, and he hurried to the kitchen.

What the hell? How could she relax now? How could she get through the rest of the night with the girls and focus on their conversation when she needed to know Gabe's thoughts? How did he see their future? Would his outlook unite with hers?

Fighting off fear and confusion, she returned to her friends.

"What happened?" Lavinia's eyes were wide with concern.

"Your aunty said something to Gabe, and he told me he'd explain later."

"Oh." Lines of disappointment creased Bean's forehead.

"I thought..." Jemma's face scrunched with surprise, as though she'd expected a very different outcome. "Things will work out how they're supposed to." She smiled, a gentle lift at the corners of her lips, her eyes clear and focused, her face blooming with serenity, with faithful conviction.

What did that mean exactly? Would Gabe remain in her life, and if so, in what capacity? She wanted to grill Jemma further, but no matter what she said, it couldn't provide a definitive answer. Only Gabe could.

The girls diverted the conversation to safer topics, and Tessa tried tuning in, but after a while, she couldn't concentrate any longer. She took in a resetting breath. "I'm sorry, ladies. Give my apologies to Tildie. I ... I need to talk to Gabe and know where I stand, where he and I stand."

"Yes. *Basta!* Enough. Go and sort things out." Lavinia gave her an encouraging smile and wrapped her in a we-support-you hug.

"Then fill us in as soon as you have a second." Bean squeezed her hand.

Jemma held Tessa's other hand and looked her in the eye. "Just be yourself."

With her friends' support bolstering her resolve,

she said goodbye and went to meet Gabe.

Twenty minutes later, she parked in his driveway.

He opened the door to his home, a cheeky, sexy smile filling her with hope. "You made it."

"I did."

He waved her forward. "Come and take a seat."

She stopped and turned to him. "Please tell me what you're thinking."

"I will." He shut the door and gestured to his comfy two-seater couch.

Unease filled her stomach with a sudden attack of acid reflux, but she did as he requested.

Gabe disappeared into his bedroom, and returned with one hand behind his back. He hesitated and searched her eyes. "You'll most likely think this is bullshit, but Zia Milla was adamant that I have the power, the gift, and reinforced for me not to be afraid.

"She said that she is always available to guide me, that the universe has decreed I am meant to live and succeed in San Destino. With you. I know you're not into this sort of thing, yes, but you asked, and I'm being truthful, upfront."

"Oh."

"Is that all you have to say?"

She shook her head, wanting to speak but still too surprised, dumbfounded.

He held her face with a big, warm hand. "Do you want to be with me?"

"I do. I've always wanted to be with you, Gabe." It didn't matter whether he did or didn't have some so-called special power. She loved him for him, and all his honesty, sincerity and heartfelt goodness.

He dropped onto one knee and grasped her hand. "My darling, I want you as my lifelong partner. I want you to be my wife. We are and always have been

Lovebirds. You know that, yes."

She stared at him with disbelief and a high dose of hope.

"I get you're not into all the spiritual stuff, but as bizarre as it sounds, Zia Milla's words were the sign I needed. It could be totally coincidental, but I don't care. I don't care what it was that brought me back to you. I'm just so grateful I'm here. I went with my gut and made the best decision of my life. We have amazing synergy, always have. I know we've only just reconnected, but … I love you. I need you."

Gabe brought his other hand forward and unfurled his fingers, revealing a platinum ring with a huge solitaire heart diamond that looked like two birds kissing. Or was that just her loving, Gabe-skewed perspective?

She gasped. "When did you—?"

"Zia Milla's words jolted me into action. But this time, I needed to make sure I did everything properly. In person. I had to get you a ring before I proposed. So, on the way home, I went past that beautiful boutique jewelry shop in Juniper Hollow before they closed, and this ring spoke to me. Made me think of you."

Ecstatic tears ran down her cheeks. She'd hoped, wished, some might say 'prayed' that he'd see their reunion as more than high-octane lust, as something solid, but hadn't been sure what would turn him around, what would make him believe in *them*.

She'd had no idea what it'd take for him to give them a serious second chance. And now that she had one, to foster it further, she needed to be less rigid and more open-minded with her beliefs as well. "You are the sweetest man. I love you too. So much."

He stayed on his knee and held her gaze with an imploring stare. "And the wife thing?"

She sniffled and laughed, potent energy buzzing

between them, and wrapped him in a super-tight hug. "I can't imagine anything better than being married to you."

A lightning bolt of love had struck her body and stayed, burning bright and sizzling inside, heating her up like the comforting, blazing heat from a bonfire. The soul-deep reaction forever changed her existence to a pure positive.

Gabe had proved it right now by acknowledging their relationship, discarding all his fear and apprehension, and proposing. By risking his heart, he'd gained hers. She'd never loved a man more.

Was he worth the wait?

Absolutely.

Chapter Ten

Beltane, 1ˢᵗ May

The wind whipped up across the bay, blowing Tessa's veil off her face, her bridal white dress off her legs, revealing her strappy white-and-silver sandals. Never hesitating, she walked toward Gabe, her husband-to-be, standing on the pier, right in front of Lovebirds.

Ready, waiting, his gaze roved over her body, the hugest adoring grin on his face.

His contagious ecstatic exuberance, mixed with her barely containable excitement, had her beaming with a big, broad reciprocal smile. She was elated beyond belief. Her stare refused to deviate from Gabe, even though her peripheral vision registered their guests smiling, waving, and cheering with exceptional enthusiasm.

Nothing could divert her attention from her prize of a soon-to-be husband. The man in question looked incredible in his family's heritage tartan kilt—the same blue as his eyes, with black check and white stripes—and a white shirt, matching tartan tie, black vest, and black tailored jacket, a decorative black sporran hanging from his hips.

She made her way slowly down the makeshift aisle, clutching her bouquet of peonies mixed with colorful flowers native to San Destino—beautifully arranged by Jemma. Close friends and family packed into neatly lined rows, the outer edges decorated with fragrant blossoming white roses and sprigs of greenery.

Gabe had thought of everything when it came to the ceremony, set up, and honeymoon. All she'd had to focus on was her dress, the flowers, and the menu. They made a great team. Always had. Nothing had changed.

Only for the better.

Lavinia took her place at the top of the aisle, near Gabe and his groomsman. She turned and grinned, her long blue dress, in the same shade as the tartan, flattering her every curve.

Tessa and Gabe had both wanted to keep their wedding a small, intimate affair, so she'd selected her best friend, Lavinia, as her maid of honor and Gabe had asked Lavinia's lawyer partner, Carter, to be his best man.

Gabe reached out and clasped Tessa's hand. "You look breathtaking, my darling."

"So do you."

She could have gotten fully immersed in Gabe, but the celebrant interrupted their little love bubble and commenced the ceremony, which flew by in a flash.

The wind stopped and the sun broke out from behind the clouds. "You may kiss the bri—"

Gabe's lips dominated hers, needy, desperate, full of desire, before the celebrant even finished his sentence. And she reciprocated, entirely captivated by her husband's spell. Had this power he supposedly possessed come into play?

Or did pure love explain her irresistible, palpable attraction to him? A combination of both, most likely. However, in the end, it didn't matter. What mattered was them creating and sustaining a strong, long-lasting bond.

Going by his response, one hand cradling her face, the other grasping her ass, he felt the intensity just as fiercely. So a supernatural element alone couldn't explain the phenomenon. Just as she'd always believed.

Freedom of choice, plus the environment as a whole had the biggest impact on shifting energy, not just some mysterious, unexplainable force. And even if a spiritual element existed, so many energies were at play, they had to interact and come together.

Just like what had happened with her and Gabe.

Whoops and cheers broke her out of her musings and her husband's addictive kiss. They'd continue where they left off later, have more time to indulge in each other once they retreated to Gabe's home in the mountains.

Given the high caliber of staff, who'd proven their quality and reliability over the opening month of Lovebirds, Gabe had arranged for him and Tessa to take an early flight to Scotland the next day, to spend a month visiting his parents and sightseeing. They planned to explore his birthplace, the countryside, and each other. She couldn't wait. She practically vibrated with eagerness. But first they had to make it through the reception.

Gabe held her hand, an untamable grin on his face, matching his wayward hair, and led her back down the aisle, with guests hanging good-luck charms on her wrist and throwing a mix of rose petals over her and her husband's heads.

They made it to the Lovebirds entrance, in between kisses, hugs, and congratulations, and the photographer stopped them to take photos. Some featuring just the two of them, some including the maid of honor and best man, and group shots with family and friends.

Finally, she and Gabe escaped inside for a much-needed celebratory drink and some finger food, and worked their way around the room, mingling with guests. The spectacular interior decorations lit up the space, yet still retained a warm, cozy, close-knit atmosphere.

Fairy lights draped from the ceiling and wound around poles and across the bar, and tealight candles dotted the centerpiece of each table. Lovebirds looked enchanting, and dare she say it, *magical*.

After they'd spoken to everyone, Gabe whisked her away to the bridal table. "Make sure you eat, my darling. You'll need your strength for tonight." Gabe's hot, insinuating whisper scorched her ear.

Tessa's heartbeat raced up to redline level. Not because she didn't know what to expect, but because she absolutely did. Her husband never failed to satisfy. One look, one word, one touch was all it took to get her going. And going. And going.

She couldn't wait to see if he'd worn anything under his kilt. Maybe she could disappear with him into his office and find out. And hopefully that would progress to a much-needed quickie.

With her body-hugging white satin and lace gown, she'd chosen not to wear lingerie or risk a visible panty and bra line. But it also meant she needed to keep her desire in check or risk a possible wet patch on the back of her dress.

Their food came—amazing as always, even without Gabe doing his head chef role—and in between courses their guests swarmed them, preventing any opportunity to sneak away. She'd even struggled to have a short bathroom break.

After cutting Zia Milla's decadent, delicious Lovebirds cake, and completing the speeches, the DJ called them up for their first dance on the created dance floor—a cleared square of timber with chairs surrounding the edge.

Thankfully, the wine plus her adrenaline had soothed her nerves enough to wipe out her anxiety. Her natural personality veered more toward reserved, whereas, although Gabe was introverted at heart, his outgoing tendencies exhibited an innate exuberance. Forthright, confident, outspoken, in the best possible way. A true leader.

Neither of them had had dancing lessons, and yet, they fit and flowed together unbelievably well. She and Gabe formed a solid partnership, him leading, her following, in sync. They complemented each other, supporting and working as a high-functioning team, which they'd always planned to do with their vision of Lovebirds.

Gabe swept her hair off her shoulder, his lips brushing the shell of her ear. "When we get back, consider yourself promoted."

Tessa pulled away enough to look him in the eye. "To what?" She wouldn't support nepotism, no matter how tempting. It created the worst kind of culture.

"Partner."

She stopped, her frock swishing about her legs. "Thank you. But I enjoy my current job."

He re-instigated a slow sway. "Why can't you do both? I currently own the place and am the head chef."

Great point. And they were married now, so it made sense. And his proposition matched perfectly with their original plan. "You're right. On both counts. How shall we seal the deal?"

"What I have in mind isn't appropriate in public."

She shivered with anticipation. So far, he'd consistently upheld his overt and covert promises of pleasure.

Their closest friends joined them on the dance floor—Lavinia and Carter, Bean and Tad, Jemma and Sebastian, Lewis and Zia Milla—and was that Frankie and Nate dancing together?

Veronica and her mysterious partner confirmed they'd come later, and Tildie had already committed to an exclusive Beltane Ball, so couldn't make the wedding. Rumor had it she and a silver-fox, Philippe, had serious eyes for each other. It really did seem like the season for reawakening romance.

In between chatting with their fellow dancing guests, Tessa and Gabe kissed and stared into each other's eyes. Their wedding rated as the undisputed highlight of her life. But she was well and truly ready to have her new husband to herself.

She ran her tongue along his neck and nipped his earlobe. "Is it home time yet?"

Gabe looked her in the eye with a smirk on his gorgeous face. "Oh yeah. Nothing better than hooking up with a beautiful horny bride. I'm the fucking luckiest man, but you know that, yes."

"You really are." She kissed him on the lips, then they made their escape through the front entrance to an awaiting car, an excited ripple running up her spine at what was to come.

The End

LOVEBIRDS

EVERNIGHT PUBLISHING ®

www.evernightpublishing.com

www.ingramcontent.com/pod-product-compliance
Lightning Source LLC
Chambersburg PA
CBHW032206190626
46810CB00018B/1891